The Big Bow Mystery

The Big Bow Mystery

By Israel Zangwill

Dybbuk Press
New York, NY
August 2006
http://www.dybbuk-press.com

Published 2006 by Dybbuk Press, LLC
 516 W 188TH Street # 25
New York, NY 10040

ISBN: 0-9766546-3-6
Long ISBN: 9780976654636
Library Control #: 2007920113

Illustrations © Justin Weber and Thien Tran
Thanks to Vanessa Littlecrow Wojtanowicz

Introduction © Tim Lieder
Cover illustration is Mark Gertler's Merry-Go-Round
painted in 1919.

Note on text: This text is taken from the story
collection "The Gray Wig" first published in 1903. "The
Big Bow Mystery" was originally published in 1891 in
serial format in The Star, followed in 1892 in novel
form. "Cheating the Gallows" was originally published
in February 1893 with illustrations by George
Hutchinson. Spellings have been Americanized.

Table of Contents

Introduction

By now, it's commonplace to say that Raymond Chandler and Dashell Hammett weren't merely writing potboilers. Modern critics have attached the "existential dread", "social parody" and "post-modern poetry" labels to their works with voracious enthusiasm.

By contrast, academic authorities express little respect for the pre-Chandler detective novel. With a master detective and puzzle plot, the Victorian detective novel seems quaint at best, imperialist and racist at worst. Yet, can we dismiss the Victorian detective novel so easily? Certainly there's more to Sir Arthur Conan Doyle's work than nifty puzzles. Miss Marple and Inspector Poirot do not enjoy frequent printings and film adaptations because 21st century audiences love Imperialism. Despite the formulaic nature, many Victorian detective novels rise above the genre clichés and still have the power to entertain and thrill. One such example is *The Big Bow Mystery*.

Written in 1891, *The Big Bow Mystery* has enjoyed frequent reissues, and three film adaptations: *The Perfect Crime* (1928), *The Crime Doctor* (1934), and *The Verdict* (1946). Stephen Knight in his survey *Crime Fiction 1800 – 2000: Death, Detection, Diversity* singles out *Big Bow Mystery* (along with Gaston Leroux's *The Mystery of the Yellow Room)* as one of the two best known crime books from the beginning of the 20th century.[1]

The Big Bow Mystery began as a serialized novel in *The Star*, an evening London daily. *The Star*, an exemplar of the informal style known as "New Journalism," commenced publication in 1888 and its circulation peaked at nearly

---

[1] Stephen Knight, *Crime Fiction 1800-2000, Detection, Death, Diversity* (Houndsmills, UK: Palgrave Macmillan, 2004), 81.

300,000. Its founder, Thomas Power O'Connor (1848-1929), founded the paper to champion the needs of working class families.[2]

The Star's social orientation and its lively journal format provided a welcoming home for the 27 year old author. Published in daily installments over a two-week period (August 22 – September 4, 1891), The Big Bow Mystery was The Star's first serial and inaugurated a tradition of serialized detective, high adventure and romantic novels. Although later works would invite readers to suggest endings or guess the killer's identity, The Big Bow Mystery's deluge of reader speculation came unsolicited.

The Big Bow Mystery stands as the first novel-length "locked room" mystery. This mystery sub-genre revolves around a murder committed in a room locked from the inside. The victim is alone. No stranger could have entered or left without detection and suicide is not a possibility. The first locked room mystery was Edgar Allen Poe's short story "Murders in Rue Morgue" (1842) to which Zangwill plays satirical homage. The genre reached its zenith with John Dickson's The Hollow Man (1935) – also known as The Three Coffins – which not only involves a murder in a locked room, but a near simultaneous murder on a neighboring street with the same revolver – and no obvious footprints.

In an era where the mystery writer designed the detective novel as a game of wits between writer and reader, the locked room mystery was particularly popular. An author requires uncommon ingenuity to devise a credible solution - especially when the author refuses to use ghosts, secret trap doors or sliding panels. When Arthur Conan Doyle solved "The Speckled Band" with a poisonous snake manipulated to slide up and down a bell rope, many readers

[2] Information on The Star is available online at
http://www.geocities.com/thestarfictionindex/the.htm

cried foul as snakes cannot hear whistles, climb ropes or even survive under the conditions of the story.[3]

However, the murder mystery does not thrive on the mystery alone. Every mystery writer uses the basic mystery formula to create something unique. This is especially true of *The Big Bow Mystery*. Since *The Big Bow Mystery* is Zangwill's first and last mystery novel, he shows no loyalty to the mystery clichés. The first thing a reader may notice is the way Israel Zangwill purposefully skews away from the Conan Doyle model. His detective is the antithesis to the romantically eccentric Sherlock Holmes. The retired inspector Grodman is a working class knucklehead addicted to fame. Beneath his gruff exterior lurks an even angrier interior. The denouement doesn't rely on Grodman's analytical abilities; in fact, he uses his abilities for blackmail purposes.

Whereas most Victorian and post-Victorian English mysteries depict the privileged class or a romanticized bohemia, Zangwill grounds his novel in the drab reality of London's working poor. In the opening chapter, Zangwill mocks the standard use of fog as a signal to spooky atmosphere in the person of Mrs. Drabdump, who automatically associates the day's bad weather with an increased gas bill.

Mrs. Drabdump and Inspector Grodman are only the first two great characters in this novel. Zangwill fills *The Big Bow Mystery* with royalist poets, philosopher inn keepers, radical socialists, Scotland Yard inspectors and polygamists.

---

[3] Cait Murph, "The Game Still Afoot," *The Atlantic* 259(3), 1987 cited in John A. Hodgson, "The Recoil of 'The Speckled Band': Detective Story and Detective Discourse," *Poetics Today*, 13:2 (1992): 310. See also Laurence M. Klauber "The Truth About the Speckled Band" *The Baker Street Journal, an Irregular Quarterly of Sherlockiana*, 3:2 (1948): 149-157. Available at http://www.sdnhm.org/history/klauber/speckled.html)

Not surprisingly, Zangwill was writing *The Big Bow Mystery* as he was completing his major work *Children of the Ghetto*. Although *Children of the Ghetto* depicts Jews in the Sholem Aleichem vein, it mirrors *The Big Bow Mystery*. Note the core paragraph from an admiring *Children of the Ghetto* review:

> It is crowded with figures, filled with the profusion only equaled by Dickens: noble figures and despicable; grotesque figures and commonplace; humorous (how humorous we cannot hope to tell) and pathetic (how pathetic we despair to describe); figures at which we laugh, figures at which we weep, figures which we fain would have been absent from the picture, figures that we know, figures that we wish we knew; spiritual figures and "men of the earth"; poets and peddlers, beggars and millionaires; Rabbis and unbelievers; gentle women and housewives; artists and artisans;[4]

A Zangwill enthusiast cannot read Mrs. Crowl complain over an ineffectual husband who never collects rent and not remember Mrs. Ansell of *Children of the Ghetto* ranting about religious men who spend their lives studying instead of working. Likewise, the extravagant poet Denzeil Cantercot of *The Big Bow Mystery* emerges from the same parasitic soil as Melchitsedek Pinchas, the extravagant Jewish poet for hire.

Because *Children of the Ghetto* is the classic Zangwill text, critics tend to ignore the pre-*Ghetto* works as the literary

---

[4] Israel Abrahams, "Children of the Ghetto," *Jewish Chronicle*, October 14, 1892, 7.

abortions of a writer still learning his craft. This assessment cannot apply to *The Big Bow Mystery*. *The Big Bow Mystery* is not only entertaining; it's also one of the truly classic Victorian detective novels. One can read this book many times, long after one knows the solution, without tedium. Israel Zangwill wrote *The Big Bow Mystery* at an exciting time in his life. A year later, Zangwill's *Children of the Ghetto* would catapult him into major literary recognition. His early rough writing was behind him. He wouldn't plagiarize himself for decades. When you read it, you'll feel the exuberance of classic Victorian writer at the top of his game.

Suggested for further reading

Abrahams, Israel. "Children of the Ghetto Review." *Jewish Chronicle*. October 14, 1892.

Bleiler, E.F. *Three Victorian Detective Novels*. 1977.

Herz Imber, Naphtali. "Israel Zangwill: In Memoriam of *The Jewish Standard*." *Jewish Exponent*. Philadelphia. February 26, 1892.

Hodgson, John A. "The Recoil of the The Speckled Band: Detective Story and Detective Discourse," *Poetics Today*. 13:2 (1992).

Klauber, Laurence M. "The Truth About The Speckled Band." *The Baker Street Journal, an Irregular Quarterly of Sherlockiana*. 3:2 (1948). – This article is available online at http://sdnhm.org/history/klauber/speckled.html

Knight, Stephen. *Crime Fiction 1800-2000: Detection, Death, Diversity*. (Houndsmills, UK: Palgrave Macmillan). 2004.

Lehman, David. *The Perfect Murder: A Study in Detection.* (Ann Arbor: University of Michigan Press). 1989.

Murph, Cait. "The Game Still Afoot," *The Atlantic.* 259:3 (1987).

Scott, Clement. "The Great Demonstration," *Theatre,* October 1, 1892.

Star Fiction. http://www.geocities.com/thestarfictionindex/the.htm

Symons, Julian *Bloody Murder: From the Detectvie Story to the Crime Novel.* (New York: The Mysterious Press). 1993.

Van Dine. "20 Rules for Detective Fiction." http://gaslight.mtroyal.ab.ca/vandine.htm.

Zangwill, Louis. "Civilization Before Herzl." *Menorah* 13. (1927).

1895 Introduction by Israel Zangwill

Of Murders and Mysteries

As this little book was written some four years ago, I feel able to review it without prejudice. A new book just hot from the brain is naturally apt to appear faulty to its begetter, but an old book has got into the proper perspective and may be praised by him without fear or favor. *The Big Bow Mystery* seems to me an excellent murder story, as murder stories go for, while as sensational as the most of them, it contains more humor and character creation than the best. Indeed, the humor is too abundant. Mysteries should be sedate and sober. There should be a pervasive atmosphere of horror and awe such as Poe manages to create. Humor is out of tone; it would be more artistic to preserve a somber note throughout. But I was a realist in those days, and in real life mysteries occur to real persons with their individual humors, and mysterious circumstances are apt to be complicated by comic.

The indispensable condition of a good mystery is that it should be able and unable to be solved by the reader, and that the writer's solution should satisfy. Many a mystery runs on breathlessly enough till the dénouement is reached, only to leave the reader with the sense of having been robbed of his breath under false pretenses. And not only must the solution be adequate, but all its data must be given in the body of the story. The author must not suddenly spring a new person or a new circumstance upon his reader at the end. Thus, if a friend were to ask me to guess who dined with him yesterday, it would be fatuous if he had in mind somebody of whom he knew I had never heard.

The only person who has ever solved *The Big Bow Mystery* is myself. This is not paradox but plain fact. For long before the book was written, I said to myself one night that no mystery-monger had ever murdered a man in a room to which there was no possible access. The puzzle was scarcely propounded ere the solution flew up and the idea lay stored in my mind till, years later, during the silly season, the editor of a popular London evening paper, anxious to let the sea serpent have a year off, asked me to provide him with a more original piece of fiction. I might have refused, but there was murder in my soul, and here was an opportunity.

I went to work seriously, though the *Morning Post* subsequently said the skit was too labored, and I succeeded at least in exciting my readers, so many of whom sent in unsolicited testimonials in the shape of solutions during the run of the story that, when it ended, the editor asked me to say something by way of acknowledgement. Thereupon, I wrote a letter to the paper, thanking the would-be solvers for their kindly attempts to help me out of the mess into which I had got the plot. I did not like to wound their feelings by saying straight out that they had failed, one and all, to hit the real murderer, just like real police, so I tried to break the truth to them in a roundabout, mendacious fashion, as thus:

To the editors of the Star:
Sir: Now that "The Big Bow Mystery" is solved to the satisfaction of at least one person, will you allow that person the use of your invaluable columns to enable him to thank the hundreds of your readers who have favored him with their kind suggestions and solutions while his tale was running and they were reading? I

ask this more especially because great credit is due to them for enabling me to end the story in a manner so satisfactory to myself. When I started it, I had, of course, no idea who had done the murder, but I was determined that no one should guess it. Accordingly, as each correspondent sent in the name of a suspect, I determined he or she should not be the guilty party. By degrees, every one of the characters got ticked off as innocent – all except one, and I had no option but to make that character the murder. I was very sorry to do this, as I rather liked that particular person, but when one has such ingenious readers, what can one do? You can't let anybody boast that he guessed aright and, in spite of the trouble of altering the plot five or six times, I feel that I have chosen the course most consistent with the dignity of my profession.

Had I been impelled by this consideration I should certainly have brought in a verdict against Mrs. Drabdump, as recommended by the reader who said that, judging by the illustration in the "Star," she must be at least seven feet high and, therefore, could easily have got on the roof and put her (proportionately) long arm down the chimney to effect the cut. I am not responsible for the artist's conception of the character. When I last saw the good lady she was under six feet, but your artist may have had later information. The "Star is always so frightfully up to date. I ought not to omit the humorous remark of a correspondent, who said: "Mortlake might have swung in some wild way from one window to another, *at any rate in a story.*" I hope my fellow writers thus satirically prodded will not demand his name, as I object to murders "at any rate in real life." Finally, a word with the legions who have taken me to task for allowing Mr. Gladstone to write over 170 words on a postcard. It is all owing to you, sir, who announced my story as containing humorous elements. I tried to put in some, and this gentle dig at the grand old correspondent's habits was intended to be one of them. However, if I *am* to be taken "at the foot of the letter" (or rather of the postcard), I may say that only today I received a postcard containing about 250 words. But this was not from Mr. Gladstone. At any rate, till Mr. Gladstone himself repudiates this postcard, I shall consider myself justified in allow it to stand in the book.

Again thanking your readers for their invaluable assistance,

Yours, etc.

Once would have imagined that nobody could take this seriously, for it is obvious that the mystery story is just the one species of story that cannot be told impromptu or altered at the last moment, seeing that it demands the most careful piecing together and the most elaborate dovetailing. Nevertheless, if you cast your joke upon the waters, you shall find it no joke after many days. This is what I read in the *Lyttleton Times*, New Zealand: "The chain of circumstantial evidence seems fairly irrefragable. From all accounts, Mr. Zangwill himself was puzzled, after carefully forging every link, how to break it. The method ultimately adopted I consider more ingenious than convincing." After that I made up my mind never to joke again, but this good intention no helps to pave the beaten path.

I Zangwill
LONDON, September 1895

NOTE

The Mystery which the author will always associate with this story is how he got through the task of writing it. It was written in a fortnight – day by day – to meet a sudden demand from the "Star," which made a "new departure" with it.

The said fortnight was further disturbed by an extraordinary combined attack of other troubles and tasks. This is no excuse for the shortcomings of the book, as it was always open to the writer to revise or suppress it. The latter function may safely be left to the public, while if the work stands – almost to a letter – as it appeared in the "Star," it is because the author cannot tell a story more than once.

The introduction of Mr. Gladstone into a fictitious scene is defended on the ground that he is largely mythical.

I.Z.

I

On a memorable morning of early December, London opened its eyes on a frigid grey mist. There are mornings when King Fog masses his molecules of carbon in serried squadrons in the city, while he scatters them tenuously in the suburbs; so that your morning train may bear you from twilight to darkness. But today the enemy's maneuvering was more monotonous. From Bow even unto Hammersmith there draggled a dull, wretched vapor, like the wraith of an impecunious suicide come into a fortune immediately after the fatal deed. The barometers and thermometers had sympathetically shared its depression, and their spirits (when they had any) were low. The cold cut like a many-bladed knife.

Mrs. Drabdump, of 11 Glover Street, Bow, was one of the few persons in London whom fog did not depress. She went about her work quite as cheerlessly as usual. She had been among the earliest to be aware of the enemy's advent, picking out the strands of fog from the coils of darkness the moment she rolled up her bedroom blind and unveiled the somber picture of the winter morning. She knew that the fog had come to stay for the day at least, and that the gas-bill for the quarter was going to beat the record in high-jumping. She also knew that this was because she had allowed her new gentleman lodger, Mr. Arthur Constant, to pay a fixed sum of a shilling a week for gas, instead of charging him a proportion of the actual account for the whole house. The meteorologists might have saved the credit of their science if they had reckoned with Mrs. Drabdump's next gas bill when they predicted the weather and made "Snow" the favorite, and said that "Fog" would be nowhere. Fog was everywhere, yet Mrs. Drabdump took no credit to herself for her prescience. Mrs. Drabdump indeed took no credit for anything, paying her way along doggedly, and struggling through life like a wearied swimmer trying to touch the horizon. That things always went as badly as she had foreseen did not exhilarate her in the least.

Mrs. Drabdump was a widow. Widows are not born but made, else you might have fancied Mrs. Drabdump had always been a widow. Nature had given her that tall, spare form, and that pale, thin-lipped, elongated, hard-eyed visage, and that painfully precise hair, which are always associated with widowhood in low life. It is only in higher circles that women can lose their husbands and yet remain bewitching. The late Mr. Drabdump had scratched the base of his thumb with a rusty nail, and Mrs. Drabdump's foreboding that he would die of lockjaw had not prevented her wrestling day and night with the shadow of Death, as she had wrestled with it vainly twice before, when Katie died of diphtheria and little Johnny of scarlet fever. Perhaps it is from overwork among the poor that Death has been reduced to a shadow.

Mrs. Drabdump was lighting the kitchen fire. She did it very scientifically, as knowing the contrariety of coal and the anxiety of flaming sticks to end in smoke unless rigidly kept up to the mark. Science was a success as usual; and Mrs. Drabdump rose from her knees content, like a Parsee priestess who had duly paid her morning devotions to her deity. Then she started violently, and nearly lost her balance. Her eye had caught the hands of the clock on the mantel. They pointed to fifteen minutes to seven. Mrs. Drabdump's devotion to the kitchen fire invariably terminated at fifteen minutes past six. What was the matter with the clock?

Mrs. Drabdump had an immediate vision of Snoppet, the neighboring horologist, keeping the clock in hand for weeks and then returning it only superficially repaired and secretly injured more vitally "for the good of the trade." The evil vision vanished as quickly as it came, exorcised by the deep boom of St. Dunstan's bells chiming the three-quarters. In its place a great horror surged. Instinct had failed; Mrs. Drabdump had risen at half-past six instead of six. Now she understood why she had been feeling so dazed and strange and sleepy. She had overslept herself.

Chagrined and puzzled, she hastily set the kettle over the crackling coal, discovering a second later that she had overslept herself because Mr. Constant wished to be woke three-quarters of an hour earlier than usual, and to have his breakfast at seven, having to speak at an early meeting of discontented tram-men. She ran at once, candle in hand, to his bedroom. It was upstairs. All "upstairs" was Arthur Constant's domain, for it consisted of but two mutually independent rooms. Mrs. Drabdump knocked viciously at the door of the one he used for a bedroom, crying, "Seven o'clock, sir. You'll be late, sir. You must get up at once." The usual slumberous "All right" was not forthcoming; but, as she herself had varied her morning salute, her ear was less expectant of the echo.

She went downstairs, with no foreboding save that the kettle would come off second best in the race between its boiling and her lodger's dressing.

For she knew there was no fear of Arthur Constant's lying deaf to the call of duty temporarily represented by Mrs. Drabdump. He was a light sleeper, and the tram-conductors' bells were probably ringing in his ears, summoning him to the meeting. Why Arthur Constant, B.A., white-handed and white-shirted, and gentleman to the very purse of him, should concern himself with tram-men when fortune had confined his necessary relations with drivers to cabmen at the least, Mrs. Drabdump could not quite make out. He probably aspired to represent Bow in Parliament; but then it would surely have been wiser to lodge with a landlady who possessed a vote by having a husband alive. Nor was there much practical wisdom in his wish to black his own boots (an occupation in which he shone but little) and to live in every way like a Bow working man. Bow working men were not so lavish in their patronage of water, whether existing in drinking glasses, morning tubs, or laundress' establishments. Nor did they eat the delicacies with which Mrs. Drabdump supplied him, with the assurance that they were the artisan's appanage. She could not bear to see him eat things unbefitting his station. Arthur Constant opened his mouth and ate what his landlady gave him, not first deliberately shutting his eyes according to the formula, the rather pluming himself on keeping them very wide open. But it is difficult for saints to see through their own halos; and in practice an aureola about the head is often indistinguishable from a mist.

The tea to be scalded in Mr. Constant's pot, when that cantankerous kettle should boil, was not the coarse mixture of black and green sacred to herself and Mr. Mortlake, of whom the thoughts of breakfast now reminded her. Poor Mr. Mortlake, gone off without any to Devonport, somewhere about four in the fog-thickened darkness of a winter night! Well, she hoped his journey would be duly rewarded, that his perks would be heavy, and that he would make as good a thing out of the "traveling expenses" as rival labor leaders roundly accused him of to other people's faces. She did not grudge him his gains, nor was it her business if, as they alleged, in introducing Mr. Constant to her vacant rooms, his idea was not merely to benefit his landlady. He had done her an uncommon good turn, queer as was the lodger thus introduced. His own apostleship to the sons of toil gave Mrs. Drabdump no twinges of perplexity. Tom Mortlake had been a compositor; and apostleship was obviously a profession better paid and of a higher social status. Tom Mortlake, the hero of a hundred strikes, set up in print on a poster, was unmistakably superior to Tom Mortlake setting up other men's names at a case. Still, the work was not all beer and skittles, and Mrs. Drabdump felt that Tom's latest job was not enviable.

She shook his door as she passed it on her way back to the kitchen, but there was no response. The street door was only a few feet off down the passage and a glance at it dispelled the last hope that Tom had abandoned the journey. The door was unbolted and unchained, and the only security was the latch-key lock. Mrs. Drabdump felt a whit uneasy, though, to give her her due, she never suffered as much as most good housewives do from criminals who never come. Not quite opposite, but still only a few doors off, on the other side of the street, lived the celebrated ex-detective Grodman, and, illogically enough, his presence in the street gave Mrs. Drabdump a curious sense of security, as of a believer living under the shadow of the fane. That any human being of ill odor should consciously come within a mile of the scent of so famous a sleuth hound seemed to her highly improbable. Grodman had retired (with a competence) and was only a sleeping dog now; still, even criminals would have sense enough to let him lie.

So Mrs. Drabdump did not really feel that there had been any danger, especially as a second glance at the street door showed that Mortlake had been thoughtful enough to slip the loop that held back the bolt of the big lock. She allowed herself another throb of sympathy for the labor leader whirling on his dreary way towards Devonport Dockyard. Not that he had told her anything of his journey beyond the town; but she knew Devonport had a Dockyard because Jessie Dymond - Tom's sweetheart – once mentioned that her aunt lived near there, and it lay on the surface that Tom had gone to help the dockers who were imitating their London brethren. Mrs. Drabdump did not need to be told things to be aware of them. She went back to prepare Mr. Constant's superfine tea, vaguely wondering why people were so discontented nowadays. But when she brought up the tea and the toast and the eggs to Mr. Constant's sitting room (which adjoined his bedroom, though without communicating with it), Mr. Constant was not sitting in it. She lit the gas, and laid the cloth; then she returned to the landing and beat at the bedroom door with an imperative palm. Silence alone answered her. She called him by name and told him the hour, but hers was the only voice she heard, and it sounded strangely to her in the shadows of the staircase. Then, muttering, "Poor gentleman, he had the toothache last night; and p'r'aps he's only just got a wink o' sleep. Pity to disturb him for the sake of them grizzling conductors. I'll let him sleep his usual time," she bore the teapot downstairs with a mournful, almost poetic, consciousness that soft-boiled eggs (like love) must grow cold.

Half past seven came and she knocked again. But Constant slept on.

His letters, always a strange assortment, arrived at eight, and a telegram came soon after. Mrs. Drabdump rattled his door, shouted and at last put the wire under it. Her heart was beating fast enough now, though there seemed to be a cold, clammy snake curling round it. She went downstairs again and turned the handle of Mortlake's room and went in without knowing why. The coverlet of the bed showed that the occupant had only lain down in his clothes, as if fearing to miss the early train. She had not for a moment expected to find him in the room; yet somehow the consciousness that she was alone in the house with the sleeping Constant seemed to flash for the first time upon her, and the clammy snake tightened its folds round her heart.

She opened the street door and her eye wandered nervously up and down. It was half-past eight. The little street stretched cold and still in the grey mist, blinking bleary eyes at either end, where the street lamps smoldered on. No one was visible for the moment, though smoke was rising from many of the chimneys to greet its sister mist. At the house of the detective across the way the blinds were still down and the shutters up. Yet the familiar, prosaic aspect of the street calmed her. The bleak air set her coughing; she slammed the door and returned to the kitchen to make fresh tea for Constant, who could only be in a deep sleep. But the canister trembled in her grasp. She did not know whether she dropped it or threw it down, but there was nothing in the hand that battered again a moment later at the bedroom door. No sound within answered the clamor without. She rained blow upon blow in a sort of spasm of frenzy, scarce remembering that her object was merely to wake her lodger, and almost staving in the lower panels with her kicks. Then she turned the handle and tried to open the door, but it was locked. The resistance recalled her to herself; she had a moment of shocked decency at the thought that she had been about to enter Constant's bedroom. Then the terror came over her afresh. She felt that she was alone in the house with a corpse. She sank to the floor, cowering; with difficulty stifling a desire to scream. Then she rose with a jerk and raced down the stairs without looking behind her, and threw open the door and ran out into the street, only pulling up with her hand violently agitating Grodman's door knocker. In a moment the first-floor window was raised - the little house was of the same pattern as her own - and Grodman's full fleshy face loomed through the fog in sleepy irritation from under a nightcap. Despite its scowl the ex-detective's face dawned upon her like the sun upon an occupant of the haunted chamber.

"What in the devil's the matter?" he growled. Grodman was not an early bird, now that he had no worms to catch. He could afford to despise proverbs now, for the house in which he lived was his, and he lived in it because several other houses in the street were also his, and it is well for the landlord to be about his own estate in Bow, where poachers often shoot the moon. Perhaps the desire to enjoy his greatness among his early cronies counted for something, too, for he had been born and bred at Bow, receiving when a youth his first engagement from the local police quarters, whence he had drawn a few shillings a week as an amateur detective in his leisure hours.

Grodman was still a bachelor. In the celestial matrimonial bureau a partner might have been selected for him, but he had never been able to discover her. It was his one failure as a detective. He was a self-sufficing person, who preferred a gas stove to a domestic; but in deference to Glover Street opinion he admitted a female factotum between 10am and

10pm, and, equally in deference to Glover Street opinion, excluded her between 10pm and 10am.

"I want you to come across at once," Mrs. Drabdump gasped. "Something has happened to Mr. Constant."

"What! Not bludgeoned by the police at the meeting this morning, I hope?"

"No, no! He didn't go. He is dead."

"Dead?" Grodman's face grew very serious now.

"Yes. Murdered!"

"What?" almost shouted the ex-detective. "How? When? Where? Who?"

"I don't know. I can't get to him. I have beaten at his door. He does not answer."

Grodman's face lit up with relief.

"You silly woman! Is that all? I shall have a cold in my head. Bitter weather. He's dog-tired after yesterday: processions, three speeches, kindergarten, lecture on 'the moon,' article on cooperation. That's his style." It was also Grodman's style. He never wasted words.

"No," Mrs. Drabdump breathed up at him solemnly, "he's dead."

"All right; go back. Don't alarm the neighborhood unnecessarily. Wait for me. Down in five minutes." Grodman did not take this Cassandra of the kitchen too seriously. Probably he knew his woman. His small, bead-like eyes glittered with an almost amused smile as he withdrew them from Mrs. Drabdump's ken, and shut down the sash with a bang. The poor woman ran back across the road and through her door, which she would not close behind her. It seemed to shut her in with the dead. She waited in the passage. After an age - seven minutes by any honest clock - Grodman made his appearance, looking as dressed as usual, but with unkempt hair and with disconsolate side-whisker. He was not quite used to that side-whisker yet, for it had only recently come within the margin of cultivation. In active service Grodman had been clean-shaven, like all members of *the* profession for surely your detective is the most versatile of actors. Mrs. Drabdump closed the street door quietly, and pointed to the stairs, fear operating like a polite desire to give him precedence. Grodman ascended, amusement still glimmering in his eyes. Arrived on the landing he knocked peremptorily at the door, crying, "Nine o'clock, Mr. Constant; nine o'clock!" When he ceased there was no other sound or movement. His face grew more serious. He waited, then knocked, and cried louder. He turned the handle but the door was fast. He tried to peer through the keyhole, but it was blocked. He shook the upper panels, but the door seemed bolted as well as locked. He stood still, his face set and rigid, for he liked and esteemed the man.

"Ay, knock your loudest," whispered the pale-faced woman. "You'll not wake him now."

The grey mist had followed them through the street door, and hovered about the staircase, charging the air with a moist sepulchral odor.

"Locked and bolted," muttered Grodman, shaking the door afresh.

"Burst it open," breathed the woman, trembling violently all over, and holding her hands before her as if to ward off the dreadful vision. Without another word, Grodman applied his shoulder to the door, and made a violent muscular effort. He had been an athlete in his time, and the sap was yet in him. The door creaked, little by little it began to give, the woodwork enclosing the bolt of the lock splintered, the panels bent inwards, the large upper bolt tore off its iron staple; the door flew back with a crash. Grodman rushed in.

"My God!" he cried. The woman shrieked. The sight was too terrible.

Within a few hours the jubilant newsboys were shrieking "Horrible Suicide in Bow," and *The Moon* poster added, for the satisfaction of those too poor to purchase, "A Philanthropist Cuts His Throat."

II

But the newspapers were premature. Scotland Yard refused to prejudice the case despite the penny-a-liners. Several arrests were made, so that the later editions were compelled to soften "Suicide" into "Mystery." The people arrested were a nondescript collection of tramps. Most of them had committed other offences for which the police had not arrested them. One bewildered looking gentleman gave himself up (as if he were a riddle) but the police would have none of him, and restored him forthwith to his friends and keepers. The number of candidates for each new opening in Newgate is astonishing.

The full significance of this tragedy of a noble young life cut short had hardly time to filter into the public mind, when a fresh sensation absorbed it. Tom Mortlake had been arrested the same day at Liverpool on suspicion of being concerned in the death of his fellow lodger. The news fell like a bombshell upon a land in which Tom Mortlake's name was a household word. That the gifted artisan orator, who had never shrunk upon occasion from launching red rhetoric at society, should actually have shed blood seemed too startling, especially as the blood shed was not blue, but the property of a lovable young middle class idealist, who had now literally given his life to the Cause. But this supplementary sensation did not grow to a head, and everybody (save a few labor leaders) was relieved to hear that Tom had been released almost immediately, being merely subpoenaed to appear at the inquest. In an interview which he accorded to the representative of a Liverpool paper the same afternoon, he stated that he put his arrest down entirely to the enmity and rancor entertained towards him by the police throughout the country. He had come to Liverpool to trace the movements of a friend about whom he was very uneasy, and he was making anxious inquiries at the docks to discover at what times steamers left for America, when the detectives stationed there had, in accordance with instructions from headquarters, arrested him as a suspicious-looking character.

"Though," said Tom, "they must very well have known my phiz, as I have been sketched and caricatured all over the shop. When I told them who I was they had the decency to let me go. They thought they'd scored off me enough, I reckon. Yes, it certainly *is* a strange coincidence that I might actually have had something to do with the poor fellow's death, which has cut me up as much as anybody; though if they had known I had just come from the 'scene of the crime,' and actually lived in the house, they would probably have let me alone." He laughed sarcastically. "They are a queer lot of muddle-heads, are the police. Their motto is, 'First catch your man, then cook the evidence.' If you're on the spot you're guilty because you're there, and if you're elsewhere you're guilty because you have gone away. Oh, I know them! If they could have seen their way to clap me in quod, they'd ha' done it. Luckily I know the number of the cabman who took me to Euston before five this morning."

"If they clapped you in quod," the interviewer reported himself as facetiously observing, "the prisoners would be on strike in a week."

"Yes, but there would be so many blacklegs ready to take their places," Mortlake flashed back, "that I'm afraid it 'ould be no go. But do excuse me. I am so upset about my friend. I'm afraid he has left England, and I have to make inquiries; and now there's poor Constant gone. Horrible! Horrible! And I'm due in London at the inquest. I must really run away. Goodbye. Tell your readers it's all a police grudge."

"One last word, Mr. Mortlake, if you please. Is it true that you were billed to preside at a great meeting of clerks at St. James's Hall between one and two today to protest against the German invasion?"

"Whew! So I was. But the beggars arrested me just before one, when I was going to wire, and then the news of poor Constant's end drove it out of my head. What a nuisance! Lord, how troubles do come together! Well, goodbye, send me a copy of the paper."

Tom Mortlake's evidence at the inquest added little beyond this to the public knowledge of his movements on the morning of the Mystery. The cabman who drove him to Euston had written indignantly to the papers to say that he picked up his celebrated fare at Bow Railway Station at about half past four a.m., and the arrest was a deliberate insult to democracy, and he offered to make an affidavit to that effect, leaving it dubious to which effect. But Scotland Yard betrayed no itch for the affidavit in question, and No. 2138 subsided again into the obscurity of his rank. Mortlake - whose face was very pale below the black mane brushed back from his fine forehead - gave his evidence in low, sympathetic tones. He had known the deceased for over a year, coming constantly across him in their common political and social work, and had found the furnished rooms for him in Glover Street at his own request, they just being to let when Constant resolved to leave his rooms at Oxford House in Bethnal Green, and to share the actual life of the people. The locality suited the deceased, as being near the People's Palace. He respected and admired the deceased, whose genuine goodness had won all hearts. The deceased was an untiring worker; never grumbled, was always in fair spirits, regarded his life and wealth as a sacred trust to be used for the benefit of humanity. He had last seen him at a quarter past 9pm on the day preceding his death. He (witness) had received a letter by the last post which made him uneasy about a friend. He went up to consult deceased about it. Deceased was evidently suffering from toothache, and was fixing a piece of cotton-wool in a hollow tooth, but he did not complain. Deceased seemed rather upset by the news he brought, and they both discussed it rather excitedly.

By a JURYMAN: Did the news concern him?

MORTLAKE: Only impersonally. He knew my friend, and was keenly sympathetic when one was in trouble.

CORONER: Could you show the jury the letter you received?

MORTLAKE: I have mislaid it, and cannot make out where it has got to. If you, sir, think it relevant or essential, I will state what the trouble was.

CORONER: Was the toothache very violent?

MORTLAKE: I cannot tell. I think not, though he told me it had disturbed his rest the night before.

CORONER: What time did you leave him?

MORTLAKE: About twenty to ten.

CORONER: And what did you do then?

MORTLAKE: I went out for an hour or so to make some inquiries. Then I returned, and told my landlady I should be leaving by an early train for - for the country.

CORONER: And that was the last you saw of the deceased?

MORTLAKE (with emotion): The last.

CORONER: How was he when you left him?

MORTLAKE: Mainly concerned about my trouble.

CORONER: Otherwise you saw nothing unusual about him?

MORTLAKE: Nothing.

CORONER: What time did you leave the house on Tuesday morning?

MORTLAKE: At about five-and-twenty minutes past four.

CORONER: Are you sure that you shut the street door?

MORTLAKE: Quite sure. Knowing my landlady was rather a timid person, I even slipped the bolt of the big lock, which was usually tied back. It was impossible for anyone to get in, even with a latch-key.

Mrs. Drabdump's evidence (which, of course, preceded his) was more important and occupied a considerable time, unduly eked out by Drabdumpian padding. Thus she not only deposed that Mr. Constant had the toothache, but that it was going to last about a week; in tragi-comic indifference to the radical cure that had been effected. Her account of the last hours of the deceased tallied with Mortlake's, only that she feared Mortlake was quarrelling with him over something in the letter that came by the nine o'clock post. Deceased had left the house a little after Mortlake, but had returned before him, and had gone straight to his bedroom. She had not actually seen him come in, having been in the kitchen, but she heard his latch-key, followed by his light step up the stairs.

A JURYMAN: How do you know it was not somebody else? (*Sensation, of which the juryman tries to look unconscious.*)

WITNESS: He called down to me over the banisters, and says in his sweetish voice, "Be hextra sure to wake me at a quarter to seven, Mrs. Drabdump, or else I shan't get to my tram meeting." (*Juryman collapses.*)

CORONER: And did you wake him?

MRS. DRABDUMP (breaking down): Oh, my lud, how can you ask?

CORONER: There, there, compose yourself. I mean did you try to wake him?

MRS. DRABDUMP: I have taken in and done for lodgers this seventeen years, my lud, and have always gave satisfaction; and Mr. Mortlake, he wouldn't ha' recommended me otherwise, though I wish to Heaven the poor gentleman had never--

CORONER: Yes, yes, of course. You tried to rouse him?

But it was some time before Mrs. Drabdump was sufficiently calm to explain that, though she had overslept herself, and though it would have been all the same anyhow, she *had* come up to time. Bit by bit the tragic story was forced from her lips - a tragedy that even her telling could not make tawdry. She told with superfluous detail how when Mr. Grodman broke in the door, she saw her unhappy gentleman lodger lying on his back in bed, stone dead, with a gaping red wound in his throat; how her stronger minded companion calmed her a little by spreading a handkerchief over the distorted face; how they then looked vainly about and under the bed for any instrument by which the deed could have been done, the veteran detective carefully making a rapid inventory of the contents of the room, and taking notes of the precise position and condition of the body before anything was disturbed by the arrival of gapers or bunglers; how she had pointed out to him that both the windows were firmly bolted to keep out the cold night air; how, having noted this down with a puzzled, pitying shake of the head, he had opened the window to summon the police, and espied in the fog one Denzil Cantercot, whom he called, and told to run to the nearest police station and ask them to send on an inspector and a surgeon; how they both remained in the room till the police arrived, Grodman pondering deeply the while and making notes every now and again, as fresh points occurred to him and asking her questions about the poor, weak-headed young man. Pressed as to what she meant by calling the deceased "weak-headed," she replied that some of her neighbors wrote him begging letters, though, Heaven knew, they were better off than herself, who had to scrape her fingers to the bone for every penny she earned. Under further pressure from Mr. Talbot, who was watching the inquiry on behalf of Arthur Constant's family, Mrs. Drabdump admitted that the deceased had behaved like a human being, nor was there anything externally eccentric or queer in his conduct. He was always cheerful and pleasant spoken, though certainly soft. God rest his soul. No; he never shaved, but wore all the hair that Heaven had given him.

By a JURYMAN: She thought deceased was in the habit of locking his door when he went to bed. Of course, she couldn't say for certain. (Laughter.) There was no need to bolt the door as well. The bolt slid upwards, and was at the top of the door. When she first let lodgings, her reasons for which she seemed anxious to publish, there had only been a bolt, but a suspicious lodger, she would not call him a gentleman, had complained that he could not fasten his door behind him, and so she had been put to the expense of having a lock made. The complaining lodger went off soon after without paying his rent. (Laughter.) She had always known he would.

The CORONER: Was deceased at all nervous?

WITNESS: No, he was a very nice gentleman. (A laugh.)

CORONER: I mean did he seem afraid of being robbed?

WITNESS: No, he was always goin' to demonstrations. (Laughter.) I told him to be careful. I told him I lost a purse with 3s. 2d. myself on Jubilee Day.

Mrs. Drabdump resumed her seat, weeping vaguely.

The CORONER: Gentlemen, we shall have an opportunity of viewing the room shortly.

The story of the discovery of the body was retold, though more scientifically, by Mr. George Grodman, whose unexpected resurgence into the realm of his early exploits excited as keen a curiosity as the reappearance "for this occasion only" of a retired prima donna. His book, *Criminals I have Caught,* passed from the twenty-third to the twenty-fourth edition merely on the strength of it. Mr. Grodman stated that the body was still warm when he found it. He thought that death was quite recent. The door he had had to burst was bolted as well as locked. He confirmed Mrs. Drabdump's statement about the windows; the chimney was very narrow. The cut looked as if done by a razor. There was no instrument lying about the room. He had known the deceased about a month. He seemed a very earnest, simple-minded young fellow, who spoke a great deal about the brotherhood of man. (The hardened old man hunter's voice was not free from a tremor as he spoke jerkily of the dead man's enthusiasms.) He should have thought the deceased the last man in the world to commit suicide.

Mr. DENZIL CANTERCOT was next called: He was a poet. (Laughter.) He was on his way to Mr. Grodman's house to tell him he had been unable to do some writing for him because he was suffering from writer's cramp, when Mr. Grodman called to him from the window of No. 11 and asked him to run for the police. No, he did not run; he was a philosopher. (Laughter.) He returned with them to the door, but did not go up. He had no stomach for crude sensations. (Laughter.) The grey fog was sufficiently unbeautiful for him for one morning. (Laughter.)

Inspector HOWLETT said: About 9.45 on the morning of Tuesday, 4th December, from information received, he went with Sergeant Runnymede and Dr. Robinson to 11 Glover Street, Bow, and there found the dead body of a young man, lying on his back with his throat cut. The door of the room had been smashed in, and the lock and the bolt evidently forced. The room was tidy. There were no marks of blood on the floor. A purse full of gold was on the dressing-table beside a big book. A hip-bath, with cold water, stood beside the bed, over which was a hanging bookcase. There was a large wardrobe against the wall next to the door. The chimney was very narrow. There were two windows, one bolted. It was about eighteen feet to the pavement. There was no way of climbing up. No one could possibly have got out of the room, and then bolted the doors and windows behind him; and he had searched all parts of the room in which anyone might have been concealed. He had been unable to find any instrument in the room in spite of exhaustive search, there being not even a penknife in the pockets of the clothes of the deceased, which lay on a chair. The house and the back yard, and the adjacent pavement, had also been fruitlessly searched.

Sergeant RUNNYMEDE made an identical statement, saving only that *he* had gone with Dr. Robinson and Inspector Howlett.

Dr. ROBINSON, divisional surgeon, said: "The deceased was lying on his back, with his throat cut. The body was not yet cold, the abdominal region being quite warm. Rigor mortis had set in in the lower jaw, neck, and upper extremities. The muscles contracted when beaten. I inferred that life had been extinct some two or three hours, probably not longer, it might have been less. The bed-clothes would keep the lower part warm for some time. The wound, which was a deep one, was five and a half inches from right to left across the throat to a point under the left ear. The upper portion of the windpipe was severed, and likewise the jugular vein. The muscular coating of the carotid artery was divided. There was a slight cut, as if in continuation of the wound, on the thumb of the left hand. The hands were clasped underneath the head. There was no blood on the right hand. The wound could not have been self-inflicted. A sharp instrument had been used, such as a razor. The cut might have been made by a left-handed person. No doubt death was practically instantaneous. I saw no signs of a struggle about the body or the room.

I noticed a purse on the dressing-table, lying next to Madame Blavatsky's big book on Theosophy. Sergeant Runnymede drew my attention to the fact that the door had evidently been locked and bolted from within."

By a JURYMAN: I do not say the cuts could not have been made by a right-handed person. I can offer no suggestion as to how the inflictor of the wound got in or out. Extremely improbable that the cut was self-inflicted. There was little trace of the outside fog in the room.

Police constable Williams said he was on duty in the early hours of the morning of the 4th inst. Glover Street lay within his beat. He saw or heard nothing suspicious. The fog was never very dense, though nasty to the throat. He had passed through Glover Street about half-past four. He had not seen Mr. Mortlake or anybody else leave the house.

The Court here adjourned; the coroner and the jury repairing in a body to 11 Glover Street, to view the house and the bedroom of the deceased. And the evening posters announced "The Bow Mystery Thickens."

III

Before the inquiry was resumed, all the poor wretches in custody had been released on suspicion that they were innocent; there was not a single case even for a magistrate. Clues, which at such seasons are gathered by the police like blackberries off the hedges, were scanty and unripe. Inferior specimens were offered them by bushels, but there was not a good one among the lot. The police could not even manufacture a clue.

Arthur Constant's death was already the theme of every hearth, railway carriage, and public house. The dead idealist had points of contact with so many spheres. The East End and the West End alike were moved and excited, the Democratic Leagues and the Churches, the Doss-houses and the Universities. The pity of it! And then the impenetrable mystery of it!

The evidence given in the concluding portion of the investigation was necessarily less sensational. There were no more witnesses to bring the scent of blood over the coroner's table; those who had yet to be heard were merely relatives and friends of the deceased, who spoke of him as he had been in life. His parents were dead, perhaps happily for them; his relatives had seen little of him, and had scarce heard as much about him as the outside world. No man is a prophet in his own country, and, even if he migrates, it is advisable for him to leave his family at home. His friends were a motley crew; friends of the same friend are not necessarily friends of one another. But their diversity only made the congruity of the tale they had to tell more striking. It was the tale of a man who had never made an enemy even by benefiting him, nor lost a friend even by refusing his favors; the tale of a man whose heart overflowed with peace and goodwill to all men all the year round; of a man to whom Christmas came not once, but three hundred and sixty-five times a year; it was the tale of a brilliant intellect, who gave up to mankind what was meant for himself, and worked as a laborer in the vineyard of humanity, never crying that the grapes were sour; of a man uniformly cheerful and of good courage, living in that forgetfulness of self which is the truest antidote to despair.

And yet there was not quite wanting the note of pain to jar the harmony and make it human. Richard Elton, his chum from boyhood, and vicar of Somerton, in Midlandshire, handed to the coroner a letter received from the deceased about ten days before his death, containing some passages which the coroner read aloud: "Do you know anything of Schopenhauer? I mean anything beyond the current misconceptions? I have been making his acquaintance lately. He is an agreeable rattle of a pessimist; his essay on 'The Misery of Mankind' is quite lively reading. At first his assimilation of Christianity and Pessimism (it occurs in his essay on 'Suicide') dazzled me as an audacious paradox. But there is truth in it. Verily the whole creation groaneth and travaileth, and man is a degraded monster, and sin is over all. Ah, my friend, I have shed many of my illusions since I came to this seething hive of misery and wrongdoing. What shall one man's life – a million men's lives - avail against the corruption, the vulgarity, and the squalor of civilization? Sometimes I feel like a farthing rush light in the Hall of Eblis. Selfishness is so long and life so short. And the worst of it is that everybody is so beastly contented. The poor no more desire comfort than the rich culture. The woman, to whom a penny school fee for her child represents an appreciable slice of her income, is satisfied that the rich we shall always have with us.

"The real old Tories are the paupers in the Workhouse. The radical working men are jealous of their own leaders, and the leaders are jealous of one another. Schopenhauer must have organized a Labor Party in his salad days. And yet one can't help feeling that he committed suicide as a philosopher by not committing it as a man. He claims kinship with Buddha, too; though Esoteric Buddhism at least seems spheres removed from the philosophy of 'the Will and the Idea.' What a wonderful woman Madame Blavatsky must be! I can't say I follow her, for she is up in the clouds nearly all the time, and I haven't as yet developed an astral body. Shall I send you on her book? It is fascinating. I am becoming quite a fluent orator. One soon gets into the way of it. The horrible thing is that you catch yourself saying things to lead up to 'Cheers' instead of sticking to the plain realities of the business. Lucy is still doing the galleries in Italy. It used to pain me sometimes to think of my darling's happiness when I came across a flat-chested factory girl. Now I feel her happiness is as important as a factory girl's."

Lucy, the witness explained, was Lucy Brent, the betrothed of the deceased. The poor girl had been telegraphed for, and had started for England. The witness stated that the outburst of despondency in this letter was almost a solitary one, most of the letters in his possession being bright, buoyant, and hopeful. Even this letter ended with a humorous statement of the writer's manifold plans and projects for the New Year. The deceased was a good Churchman.

CORONER: Was there any private trouble in his own life to account for the temporary despondency?

WITNESS: Not so far as I am aware. His financial position was exceptionally favorable.

CORONER: There had been no quarrel with Miss Brent?

WITNESS: I have the best authority for saying that no shadow of difference had ever come between them.

CORONER: Was the deceased left-handed?

WITNESS: Certainly not. He was not even ambidexter.

A JURYMAN: Isn't Shoppinhour one of the infidel writers, published by the Freethought Publication Society?

WITNESS: I do not know who publishes his books.

The JURYMAN (a small grocer and big raw-boned Scotchman, rejoicing in the name of Sandy Sanderson and the dignities of deaconry and membership of the committee of the Bow Conservative Association): No equeevocation, sir. Is he not a secularist, who has lectured at the Hall of Science?

WITNESS: No, he is a foreign writer (Mr. Sanderson was heard to thank heaven for this small mercy) who believes that life is not worth living.

The JURYMAN: Were you not shocked to find the friend of a meenister reading such impure leeterature?

WITNESS: The deceased read everything. Schopenhauer is the author of a system of philosophy,

46

and not what you seem to imagine. Perhaps you would like to inspect the book? (Laughter.)

The JURYMAN: I would na' touch it with a pitchfork. Such books should be burnt. And this Madame Blavatsky's book - what is that? Is that also pheelosophy?

WITNESS: No. It is Theosophy. (Laughter.)

Mr. Allan Smith, secretary of the Tram-men's Union, stated that he had had an interview with the deceased on the day before his death, when he (the deceased) spoke hopefully of the prospects of the movement, and wrote him out a check for ten guineas for his Union. Deceased promised to speak at a meeting called for a quarter past seven a.m. the next day.

Mr. Edward Wimp, of the Scotland Yard Detective Department, said that the letters and papers of the deceased threw no light upon the manner of his death, and they would be handed back to the family. His Department had not formed any theory on the subject.

The coroner proceeded to sum up the evidence. "We have to deal, gentlemen," he said, "with a most incomprehensible and mysterious case, the details of which are yet astonishingly simple. On the morning of Tuesday, the 4th inst., Mrs. Drabdump, a worthy hard-working widow, who lets lodgings at 11 Glover Street, Bow, was unable to arouse the deceased, who occupied the entire upper floor of the house. Becoming alarmed, she went across to fetch Mr. George Grodman, a gentleman known to us all by reputation, and to whose clear and scientific evidence we are much indebted, and got him to batter in the door. They found the deceased lying back in bed with a deep wound in his throat. Life had only recently become extinct. There was no trace of any instrument by which the cut could have been effected: there was no trace of any person who could have effected the cut. No person could apparently have got in or out. The medical evidence goes to show that the deceased could not have inflicted the wound himself. And yet, gentlemen, there are, in the nature of things, two - and only two - alternative explanations of his death. Either the wound was inflicted by his own hand, or it was inflicted by another's. I shall take each of these possibilities separately."

"First, did the deceased commit suicide? The medical evidence says deceased was lying with his hands clasped behind his head. Now the wound was made from right to left, and terminated by a cut on the left thumb. If the deceased had made it he would have had to do it with his right hand, while his left hand remained under his head - a most peculiar and unnatural position to assume. Moreover, in making a cut with the right hand, one would naturally move the hand from left to right. It is unlikely that the deceased would move his right hand so awkwardly and unnaturally, unless, of course, his object was to baffle suspicion. Another point is that on this hypothesis, the deceased would have had to replace his right hand beneath his head. But Dr. Robinson believes that death was instantaneous. If so, deceased could have had no time to pose so neatly. It is just possible the cut was made with the left hand, but then the deceased was right-handed. The absence of any signs of a possible weapon undoubtedly goes to corroborate the medical evidence. The police have made an exhaustive search in all places where the razor or other weapon or instrument might by any possibility have been concealed, including the bed clothes, the mattress, the pillow, and the street into which it might have been dropped. But all theories involving the willful concealment of the fatal instrument have to reckon with the fact or probability that death was instantaneous, also with the fact that there was no blood about the floor. Finally, the instrument used was in all likelihood a razor, and the deceased did not shave, and was never known to be in possession of any such instrument. If, then, we were to confine ourselves to the medical and police evidence, there would, I think, be little hesitation in dismissing the idea of suicide."

"Nevertheless, it is well to forget the physical aspect of the case for a moment and to apply our minds to an unprejudiced inquiry into the mental aspect of it. Was there any reason why the deceased should wish to take his own life? He was young, wealthy, and popular, loving and loved; life stretched fair before him. He had no vices. Plain living, high thinking, and noble doing were the three guiding stars of his life. If he had had ambition, an illustrious public career was within his reach. He was an orator of no mean power, a brilliant and industrious man. His outlook was always on the future – he was always sketching out ways in which he could be useful to his fellow-men. His purse and his time were ever at the command of whosoever could show fair claim upon them. If such a man were likely to end his own life, the science of human nature would be at an end. Still, some of the shadows of the picture have been presented to us. The man had his moments of despondency - as which of us has not? But they seem to have been few and passing. Anyhow, he was cheerful enough on the day before his death. He was suffering, too, from toothache. But it does not seem to have been violent, nor did he complain. Possibly, of course, the pain became very acute in the night. Nor must we forget that he may have overworked himself, and got his nerves into a morbid state. He worked very hard, never rising later than half past seven, and doing far more than the professional 'labor leader.' He taught, and wrote, as well as spoke and organized. But on the other hand all witnesses agreed that he was looking forward eagerly to the meeting of tram-men on the morning of the 4th inst. His whole heart was in the movement. Is it likely that this was the night he would choose for quitting the scene of his usefulness? Is it likely that if he had chosen it, he would not have left letters and a statement behind, or made a last will and testament? Mr. Wimp has found no possible clue to such conduct in his papers. Or is it likely he would have concealed the instrument? The only positive sign of intention is the bolting of his door in addition to the usual locking of it, but one cannot lay much stress on that. Regarding the mental aspects alone, the balance is largely against suicide; looking at the physical aspects, suicide is well-nigh impossible. Putting the two together, the case against suicide is all but mathematically complete. The answer, then, to our first question, "Did the deceased commit suicide?" is, that he did not."

The coroner paused, and everybody drew a long breath. The lucid exposition had been followed with admiration. If the coroner had stopped now, the jury would have unhesitatingly returned a verdict of "murder." But the coroner swallowed a mouthful of water and went on.

"We now come to the second alternative. Was the deceased the victim of homicide? In order to answer that question in the affirmative it is essential that we should be able to form some conception of the modus operandi. It is all very well for Dr. Robinson to say the cut was made by another hand; but in the absence of any theory as to how the cut could possibly have been made by that other hand, we should be driven back to the theory of self-infliction, however improbable it may seem to medical gentlemen. Now, what are the facts? When Mrs. Drabdump and Mr. Grodman found the body it was yet warm, and Mr. Grodman, a witness fortunately qualified by special experience, states that death had been quite recent. This tallies closely enough with the view of Dr. Robinson, who, examining the body about an hour later, put the time of death at two or three hours before, say seven o'clock. Mrs. Drabdump had attempted to wake the deceased at a quarter to seven, which would put back the act to a little earlier. As I understand from Dr. Robinson, that it is impossible to fix the time very precisely, death may have very well taken place several hours before Mrs. Drabdump's first attempt to wake deceased. Of course, it may have taken place between the first and second calls, as he may merely have been sound asleep at first; it may also not impossibly have taken place considerably earlier than the first call, for all the physical data seem to prove. Nevertheless, on the whole, I think we shall be least likely to err if we assume the time of death to be half past six. Gentlemen, let us picture to ourselves No. 11 Glover Street, at half-past six. We have seen the house; we know exactly how it is constructed. On the ground floor a front room tenanted by Mr. Mortlake, with two windows giving on the street, both securely bolted; a back room occupied by the landlady; and a kitchen. Mrs. Drabdump did not leave her bedroom till half-past six, so that we may be sure all the various doors and windows have not yet been unfastened; while the season of the year is a guarantee that nothing had been left open. The front door, through which Mr. Mortlake has gone out before half-past four, is guarded by the latchkey lock and the big lock. On the upper floor are two rooms - a front room used by deceased for a bedroom, and a back room which he used as a sitting-room. The back room has been left open, with the key inside, but the window is fastened. The door of the front room is not only locked but bolted. We have seen the splintered mortice and the staple of the upper bolt violently forced from the woodwork and resting on the pin. The windows are bolted, the fasteners being firmly fixed in the catches. The chimney is too narrow to admit of the passage of even a child. This room, in fact, is as firmly barred in as if besieged. It has no communication with any other part of the house. It is as absolutely self-centered and isolated as if it were a fort in the sea or a log-hut in the forest. Even if any strange person is in the house, nay, in the very sitting room of the deceased, he cannot get into the bedroom, for the house is one built for the poor, with no communication between the different rooms, so that separate families, if need be, may inhabit each. Now, however, let us grant that some person has achieved the miracle of getting into the front room, first floor, 18 feet from the ground. At half-past six, or thereabouts, he cuts the throat of the sleeping occupant. How is he then to get out without attracting the attention of the now roused landlady? But let us concede him that miracle, too. How is he to go away and yet leave the doors and windows locked and bolted from within? This is a degree of miracle at which my credulity must draw the line. No, the room had been closed all night--there is scarce a trace of fog in it. No one could get in or out. Finally, murders do not take place without motive. Robbery and revenge are the only conceivable motives. The deceased had not an enemy in the world; his money and valuables were left untouched. Everything was in order. There were no signs of a struggle. The answer, then, to our second inquiry, "Was the deceased killed by another person?" is, that he was not.

"Gentlemen, I am aware that this sounds impossible and contradictory. But it is the facts that contradict themselves. It seems clear that the deceased did not commit suicide. It seems equally clear that the deceased was not murdered. There is nothing for it, therefore, gentlemen, but to return a verdict tantamount to an acknowledgment of our incompetence to come to any adequately grounded conviction whatever as to the means or the manner by which the deceased met his death. It is the most inexplicable mystery in all my experience." (Sensation.)

The FOREMAN (after a colloquy with Mr. Sandy Sanderson): We are not agreed, sir. One of the jurors insists on a verdict of "Death from visitation by the act of God."

IV

But Sandy Sanderson's burning solicitude to fix the crime flickered out in the face of opposition, and in the end he bowed his head to the inevitable "open verdict." Then the floodgates of inkland were opened, and the deluge pattered for nine days on the deaf coffin where the poor idealist moldered. The tongues of the Press were loosened, and the leader writers reveled in recapitulating the circumstances of "The Big Bow Mystery," though they could contribute nothing but adjectives to the solution. The papers teemed with letters - it was a kind of Indian summer of the silly season. But the editors could not keep them out, nor cared to. The mystery was the one topic of conversation everywhere - it was on the carpet and the bare boards alike, in the kitchen and the drawing room. It was discussed with science or stupidity, with aspirates or without. It came up for breakfast with the rolls, and was swept off the supper table with the last crumbs.

No. 11 Glover Street, Bow, remained for days a shrine of pilgrimage. The once sleepy little street buzzed from morning till night. From all parts of the town people came to stare up at the bedroom window and wonder with a foolish face of horror. The pavement was often blocked for hours together, and itinerant vendors of refreshment made it a new market center, while vocalists hastened thither to sing the delectable ditty of the deed without having any voice in the matter. It was a pity the Government did not erect a toll gate at either end of the street. But Chancellors of the Excheckr rarely avail themselves of the more obvious expedients for paying off the National Debt.

Finally, familiarity bred contempt, and the wits grew facetious at the expense of the Mystery. Jokes on the subject appeared even in the comic papers. To the proverb, "You must not say Bo to a goose," one added, "or else she will explain you the Mystery." The name of the gentleman who asked whether the Bow Mystery was not 'arrowing shall not be divulged. There was more point in "Dagonet's" remark that, if he had been one of the unhappy jurymen, he should have been driven to suicide. A professional paradox monger pointed triumphantly to the somewhat similar situation in "the murder in the Rue Morgue," and said that Nature had been plagiarizing again - like the monkey she was - and he recommended Poe's publishers to apply for an injunction. More seriously, Poe's solution was re-suggested by "Constant Reader" as an original idea. He thought that a small organ grinder's monkey might have got down the chimney with its master's razor, and, after attempting to shave the occupant of the bed, have returned the way it came. This idea created considerable sensation, but a correspondent with a long train of letters draggling after his name pointed out that a monkey small enough to get down so narrow a flue would not be strong enough to inflict so deep a wound. This was disputed by a third writer, and the contest raged so keenly about the power of monkeys' muscles that it was almost taken for granted that a monkey was the guilty party. The bubble was pricked by the pen of "Common Sense," who laconically remarked that no traces of soot or blood had been discovered on the floor, or on the nightshirt, or the counterpane. The *Lancet's* leader on the Mystery was awaited with interest.

It said: "We cannot join in the praises that have been showered upon the coroner's summing up. It shows again the evils resulting from having coroners who are not medical men. He seems to have appreciated but inadequately the significance of the medical evidence. He should certainly have directed the jury to return a verdict of murder on that. What was it to do with him that he could see no way by which the wound could have been inflicted by an outside agency? It was for the police to find how that was done. Enough that it was impossible for the unhappy young man to have inflicted such a wound, and then to have strength and will power enough to hide the instrument and to remove perfectly every trace of his having left the bed for the purpose."

It is impossible to enumerate all the theories propounded by the amateur detectives, while Scotland Yard religiously held its tongue. Ultimately the interest on the subject became confined to a few papers which had received the best letters. Those papers that couldn't get interesting letters stopped the correspondence and sneered at the "sensationalism" of those that could. Among the mass of fantasy there were not a few notable solutions, which failed brilliantly, like rockets posing as fixed stars. One was that in the obscurity of the fog the murderer had ascended to the window of the bedroom by means of a ladder from the pavement. He had then with a diamond cut one of the panes away, and affected an entry through the aperture. On leaving he fixed in the pane of glass again (or another which he had brought with him) and thus the room remained with its bolts and locks untouched. On its being pointed out that the panes were too small, a third correspondent showed that that didn't matter, as it was only necessary to insert the hand and undo the fastening, when the entire window could be opened, the process being reversed by the murderer on leaving. This pretty edifice of glass was smashed by a glazier, who wrote to say that a pane could hardly be fixed in from only one side of a window frame, that it would fall out when touched, and that in any case the wet putty could not have escaped detection.

A door panel sliced out and replaced was also put forward, and as many trap-doors and secret passages were ascribed to No. 11 Glover Street, as if it were a mediaeval castle. Another of these clever theories was that the murderer was in the room the whole time the police were there - hidden in the wardrobe. Or he had got behind the door when Grodman broke it open, so that he was not noticed in the excitement of the discovery, and escaped with his weapon at the moment when Grodman and Mrs. Drabdump were examining the window fastenings.

Scientific explanations also were to hand to explain how the assassin locked and bolted the door behind him. Powerful magnets outside the door had been used to turn the key and push the bolt within. Murderers armed with magnets loomed on the popular imagination like a new microbe. There was only one defect in this ingenious theory - the thing could not be done. A physiologist recalled the conjurers who swallow swords - by an anatomical peculiarity of the throat - and said that the deceased might have swallowed the weapon after cutting his own throat. This was too much for the public to swallow.

As for the idea that the suicide had been affected with a penknife or its blade, or a bit of steel, which had then got buried in the wound, not even the quotation of Shelley's line: "Makes such a wound, the knife is lost in it," could secure it a moment's acceptance. The same reception was accorded to the idea that the cut had been made with a candlestick (or other harmless necessary bedroom article) constructed like a sword stick. Theories of this sort caused a humorist to explain that the deceased had hidden the razor in his hollow tooth! Some kind friend of Messrs. Maskelyne and Cook suggested that they were the only persons who could have done the deed, as no one else could get out of a locked cabinet. But perhaps the most brilliant of these flashes of false fire was the facetious, yet probably half-seriously meant letter that appeared in the *Pell Mell Press* under the heading of:

THE BIG BOW MYSTERY SOLVED

Sir,

You will remember that when the Whitechapel murders were agitating the universe, I suggested that the district coroner was the assassin. My suggestion has been disregarded. The coroner is still at large. So is the Whitechapel murderer. Perhaps this suggestive coincidence will incline the authorities to pay more attention to me this time. The problem seems to be this. The deceased could not have cut his own throat. The deceased could not have had his throat cut for him. As one of the two must have happened, this is obvious nonsense. As this is obvious nonsense I am justified in disbelieving it. As this obvious nonsense was primarily put in circulation by Mrs. Drabdump and Mr. Grodman, I am justified in disbelieving *them*. In short, sir, what guarantee have we that the whole tale is not a cock-and-bull story, invented by the two persons who first found the body? What proof is there that the deed was not done by these persons themselves, who then went to work to smash the door and break the locks and the bolts, and fasten up all the windows before they called the police in?

I enclose my card, and am, sir, yours truly,

One Who Looks Through His Own Spectacles

[Our correspondent's theory is not so audaciously original as he seems to imagine. Has he not looked through the spectacles of the people who persistently suggested that the Whitechapel murderer was invariably the policeman who found the body? *Somebody* must find the body, if it is to be found at all.

- Ed. P.M.P.]

The editor had reason to be pleased that he inserted this letter, for it drew the following interesting communication from the great detective himself:

THE BIG BOW MYSTERY SOLVED

Sir,

I do not agree with you that your correspondent's theory lacks originality. On the contrary, I think it is delightfully original. In fact it has given me an idea. What that idea is I do not yet propose to say, but if 'One who looks through his own spectacles' will favor me with his name and address I shall be happy to inform him a little before the rest of the world whether his germ has borne any fruit. I feel he is a kindred spirit, and take this opportunity of saying publicly that I was extremely disappointed at the unsatisfactory verdict. The thing was a palpable assassination; an open verdict has a tendency to relax the exertions of Scotland Yard. I hope I shall not be accused of immodesty, or of making personal reflections, when I say that the Department has had several notorious failures of late. It is not what it used to be. Crime is becoming impertinent. It no longer knows its place, so to speak. It throws down the gauntlet where once it used to cower in its fastnesses. I repeat, I make these remarks solely in the interest of law and order. I do not for one moment believe that Arthur Constant killed himself, and if Scotland Yard satisfies itself with that explanation, and turns on its other side and goes to sleep again then, sir, one of the foulest and most horrible crimes of the century will for ever go unpunished.

My acquaintance with the unhappy victim was but recent; still, I saw and knew enough of the man to be certain (and I hope I have seen and known enough of other men to judge) that he was a man constitutionally incapable of committing an act of violence, whether against himself or anybody else. He would not hurt a fly, as the saying goes. And a man of that gentle stamp always lacks the active energy to lay hands on himself. He was a man to be esteemed in no common degree, and I feel proud to be able to say that he considered me a friend. I am hardly at the time of life at which a man cares to put on his harness again; but, sir, it is impossible that I should ever know a day's rest till the perpetrator of this foul deed is discovered. I have already put myself in communication with the family of the victim, who, I am pleased to say, have every confidence in me, and look to me to clear the name of their unhappy relative from the semi-imputation of suicide. I shall be pleased if any one who shares my distrust of the authorities, and who has any clue whatever to this terrible mystery or any plausible suggestion to offer, if, in brief, any 'One who looks through his own spectacles' will communicate with me.

If I were asked to indicate the direction in which new clues might be most usefully sought, I should say, in the first instance, anything is valuable that helps us to piece together a complete picture of the manifold activities of the man in the East End. He entered one way or another into the lives of a good many people; is it true that he nowhere made enemies? With the best intentions a man may wound or offend; his interference may be resented; he may even excite jealousy. A young man like the late Mr. Constant could not have had as much practical sagacity as he had goodness. Whose corns did he tread on? The more we know of the last few months of his life the more we shall know of the manner of his death.

Thanking you by anticipation for the insertion of this letter in your valuable columns, I am, sir, yours truly,

George Grodman.
46 Glover Street, Bow.

P. S. Since writing the above lines, I have, by the kindness of Miss Brent, been placed in possession of a most valuable letter, probably the last letter written by the unhappy gentleman. It is dated Monday, 3 December, the very eve of the murder, and was addressed to her at Florence, and has now, after some delay, followed her back to London where the sad news unexpectedly brought her. It is a letter couched, on the whole, in the most hopeful spirit, and speaks in detail of his schemes.

Of course there are things in it not meant for the ears of the public, but there can be no harm in transcribing an important passage:

"You seem to have imbibed the idea that the East End is a kind of Golgotha, and this despite that the books out of which you probably got it are carefully labeled "Fiction." Lamb says somewhere that we think of the "Dark Ages" as literally without sunlight, and so I fancy people like you, dear, think of the "East End" as a mixture of mire, misery, and murder. How's that for alliteration? Why, within five minutes' walk of me there are the loveliest houses, with gardens back and front, inhabited by very fine people and furniture. Many of my university friends' mouths would water if they knew the income of some of the shopkeepers in the High Road.

"The rich people about here may not be so fashionable as those in Kensington and Bayswater, but they are every bit as stupid and materialistic. I don't deny, Lucy, I *do* have my black moments, and I do sometimes pine to get away from all this to the lands of sun and lotus eating. But, on the whole, I am too busy even to dream of dreaming. My real black moments are when I doubt if I am really doing any good. But yet on the whole my conscience or my self-conceit tells me that I am. If one cannot do much with the mass, there is at least the consolation of doing good to the individual. And, after all, is it not enough to have been an influence for good over one or two human souls? There are quite fine characters hereabout, especially in the women, natures capable not only of self-sacrifice, but of delicacy of sentiment. To have learnt to know of such, to have been of service to one or two of such - is not this ample return? I could not get to St. James's Hall to hear your friend's symphony at the Henschel concert. I have been reading Mme. Blavatsky's latest book, and getting quite interested in occult philosophy. Unfortunately I have to do all my reading in bed, and I don't find the book as soothing a soporific as most new books. For keeping one awake I find Theosophy as bad as toothache..."

THE BIG BOW MYSTERY SOLVED

Sir,

I wonder if any one besides myself has been struck by the incredible bad taste of Mr. Grodman's letter in your last issue. That he, a former servant of the Department, should publicly insult and run it down can only be charitably explained by the supposition that his judgment is failing him in his old age. In view of this letter, are the relatives of the deceased justified in entrusting him with any private documents? It is, no doubt, very good of him to undertake to avenge one whom he seems snobbishly anxious to claim as a friend; but, all things considered, should not his letter have been headed 'The Big Bow Mystery Shelved'? I enclose my card, and am, sir,

Your obedient servant,
Scotland Yard.

George Grodman read this letter with annoyance, and crumpling up the paper, murmured scornfully, "Edward Wimp!"

V

"Yes, but what will become of the Beautiful?" said Denzil Cantercot.

"Hang the Beautiful!" said Peter Crowl, as if he were on the committee of the Academy. "Give me the True."

Denzil did nothing of the sort. He didn't happen to have it about him.

Denzil Cantercot stood smoking a cigarette in his landlord's shop, and imparting an air of distinction and an agreeable aroma to the close leathery atmosphere. Crowl cobbled away, talking to his tenant without raising his eyes. He was a small, big-headed, sallow, sad-eyed man, with a greasy apron. Denzil was wearing a heavy overcoat with a fur collar. He was never seen without it in public during the winter. In private he removed it and sat in his shirt sleeves. Crowl was a thinker, or thought he was - which seems to involve original thinking anyway. His hair was thinning rapidly at the top, as if his brain was struggling to get as near as possible to the realities of things. He prided himself on having no fads. Few men are without some foible or hobby; Crowl felt almost lonely at times in his superiority. He was a Vegetarian, a Secularist, a Blue Ribbonite, a Republican, and an Anti-tobacconist. Meat was a fad. Drink was a fad. Religion was a fad. Monarchy was a fad. Tobacco was a fad. "A plain man like me," Crowl used to say, "can live without fads."

"A plain man" was Crowl's catchword. When of a Sunday morning he stood on Mile End Waste, which was opposite his shop, and held forth to the crowd on the evils of kings, priests, and mutton chops, the "plain man" turned up at intervals like the "theme" of a symphonic movement. "I am only a plain man and I want to know." It was a phrase that sabred the spider webs of logical refinement, and held them up scornfully on the point. When Crowl went for a little recreation in Victoria Park on Sunday afternoons, it was with this phrase that he invariably routed the supernaturalists.

Crowl knew his Bible better than most ministers, and always carried a minutely printed copy in his pocket, dog's-eared to mark contradictions in the text. The second chapter of Jeremiah says one thing; the first chapter of Corinthians says another. Two contradictory statements *may* both be true, but "I am only a plain man, and I want to know." Crowl spent a large part of his time in setting "the word against the word." Cock fighting affords its votaries no acuter pleasure than Crowl derived from setting two texts by the ears. Crowl had a metaphysical genius which sent his Sunday morning disciples frantic with admiration, and struck the enemy dumb with dismay. He had discovered, for instance, that the Deity could not move, owing to already filling all space. He was also the first to invent, for the confusion of the clerical, the crucial case of a saint dying at the Antipodes contemporaneously with another in London. Both went skyward to heaven, yet the two traveled in directly opposite directions. In all eternity they would never meet. Which, then, got to heaven? Or was there no such place? "I am only a plain man, and I want to know."

Preserve us our open spaces; they exist to testify to the incurable interest of humanity in the Unknown and the Misunderstood. Even 'Arry is capable of five minutes' attention to speculative theology, if 'Arriet isn't in a 'urry.

Peter Crowl was not sorry to have a lodger like Denzil Cantercot who, though a man of parts and thus worth powder and shot, was so hopelessly wrong on all subjects under the sun. In only one point did Peter Crowl agree with Denzil Cantercot - he admired Denzil Cantercot secretly. When he asked him for the True, which was about twice a day on the average, he didn't really expect to get it from him. He knew that Denzil was a poet.

"The Beautiful," he went on, "is a thing that only appeals to men like you. The True is for all men. The majority have the first claim. Till then you poets must stand aside. The True and the Useful - that's what we want. The Good of Society is the only test of things. Everything stands or falls by the Good of Society."

"The Good of Society!" echoed Denzil, scornfully. "What's the good of Society? The Individual is before all. The mass must be sacrificed to the Great Man. Otherwise the Great Man will be sacrificed to the mass. Without great men there would be no art. Without art life would be a blank."

"Ah, but we should fill it up with bread and butter," said Peter Crowl.

"Yes, it is bread and butter that kills the Beautiful," said Denzil Cantercot, bitterly. "Many of us start by following the butterfly through the verdant meadows, but we turn aside..."

"To get the grub," chuckled Peter, cobbling away.

"Peter, if you make a jest of everything, I'll not waste my time on you."

Denzil's wild eyes flashed angrily. He shook his long hair. Life was very serious to him. He never wrote comic verse intentionally.

There are three reasons why men of genius have long hair. One is: that they forget it is growing. The second is: that they like it. The third is: that it comes cheaper; they wear it long for the same reason that they wear their hats long.

Owing to this peculiarity of genius, you may get quite a reputation for lack of twopence. The economic reason did not apply to Denzil, who could always get credit with the profession on the strength of his appearance. Therefore, when Street Arabs vocally commanded him to get his hair cut, they were doing no service to barbers. Why does all the world watch over barbers and conspire to promote their interests? Denzil would have told you it was not to serve the barbers, but to gratify the crowd's instinctive resentment of originality. In his palmy days Denzil had been an editor, but he no more thought of turning his scissors against himself than of swallowing his paste. The efficacy of hair has changed since the days of Samson, otherwise Denzil would have been a Hercules instead of a long, thin, nervous man, looking too brittle and delicate to be used even for a pipe-cleaner. The narrow oval of his face sloped to a pointed, untrimmed beard. His linen was reproachable, his dingy boots were down at heel, and his cocked hat was drab with dust. Such are the effects of a love for the Beautiful.

Peter Crowl was impressed with Denzil's condemnation of flippancy, and he hastened to turn off the joke.

"I'm quite serious," he said. "Butterflies are no good to nothing or nobody; caterpillars at least save the birds from starving."

"Just like your view of things, Peter," said Denzil. "Good morning, madam." This to Mrs. Crowl, to whom he removed his hat with elaborate courtesy.

Mrs. Crowl grunted and looked at her husband with a note of interrogation in each eye. For some seconds Crowl stuck to his last, endeavoring not to see the question. He shifted uneasily on his stool. His wife coughed grimly. He looked up, saw her towering over him, and helplessly shook his head in a horizontal direction. It was wonderful how Mrs. Crowl towered over Mr. Crowl, even when he stood up in his shoes. She measured half an inch less. It was quite an optical illusion.

"Mr. Crowl," said Mrs. Crowl, "then I'll tell him."

"No, no, my dear, not yet," faltered Peter, helplessly; "leave it to me."

"I've left it to you long enough. You'll never do nothing. If it was a question of provin' to a lot of chuckleheads that Jollygee and Genesis, or some other dead and gone Scripture folk that don't consarn no mortal soul, used to contradict each other, your tongue'ud run thirteen to the dozen. But when it's a matter of takin' the bread out o' the mouths o' your own children, you ain't got no more to say for yourself than a lamppost. Here's a man stayin' with you for weeks and weeks - eatin' and drinkin' the flesh off your bones - without payin' a far--"

"Hush, hush, mother; it's all right," said poor Crowl, red as fire.

Denzil looked at her dreamily. "Is it possible you are alluding to me, Mrs. Crowl?" he said.

"Who then should I be alludin' to, Mr. Cantercot? Here's seven weeks come and gone, and not a blessed 'aypenny have I--"

"My dear Mrs. Crowl," said Denzil, removing his cigarette from his mouth with a pained air, "why reproach *me* for *your* neglect?"

"*My* neglect! I like that!"

"I don't," said Denzil more sharply. "If you had sent me in the bill you would have had the money long ago. How do you expect me to think of these details?"

"We ain't so grand down here. People pays their way. They don't get no *bills*," said Mrs. Crowl, accentuating the word with infinite scorn.

Peter hammered away at a nail, as though to drown his spouse's voice.

"It's three pounds fourteen and eightpence, if you're so anxious to know," Mrs. Crowl resumed. "And there ain't a woman in the Mile End Road as 'ud a-done it cheaper, with bread at fourpence threefarden a quartern and landlords clamburin' for rent every Monday morning almost afore the sun's up and folks draggin' and slidderin' on till their shoes is only fit to throw after brides and Christmas comin' and sevenpence a week for schoolin'!"

Peter winced under the last item. He had felt it coming like Christmas. His wife and he parted company on the question of Free Education. Peter felt that, having brought nine children into the world, it was only fair he should pay a penny a week for each of those old enough to bear educating. His better half argued that, having so many children, they ought in reason to be exempted. Only people who had few children could spare the penny. But the one point on which the cobbler-skeptic of the Mile End Road got his way was this of the fees. It was a question of conscience, and Mrs. Crowl had never made application for their remission, though she often slapped her children in vexation instead. They were used to slapping, and when nobody else slapped them they slapped one another. They were bright, ill-mannered brats, who pestered their parents and worried their teachers, and were as happy as the Road was long.

"Bother the school fees!" Peter retorted, vexed. "Mr. Cantercot's not responsible for your children."

"I should hope not, indeed, Mr. Crowl," Mrs. Crowl said sternly. "I'm ashamed of you." And with that she flounced out of the shop into the back parlor.

"It's all right," Peter called after her soothingly. "The money'll be all right, mother."

In lower circles it is customary to call your wife your mother; in somewhat superior circles it is the fashion to speak of her as "the wife," as you speak of "the Stock Exchange," or "the Thames," without claiming any peculiar property. Instinctively men are ashamed of being moral and domesticated.

Denzil puffed his cigarette, unembarrassed. Peter bent attentively over his work, making nervous stabs with his awl. There was a long silence. An organ-grinder played a waltz outside, unregarded; and, failing to annoy anybody, moved on. Denzil lit another cigarette. The dirty-faced clock on the wall chimed twelve.

"What do you think," said Crowl, "of Republics?"

"They are low," Denzil replied. "Without a Monarch there is no visible incarnation of Authority."

"What! Do you call Queen Victoria visible?"

"Peter, do you want to drive me from the house? Leave frivolousness to women, whose minds are only large enough for domestic difficulties. Republics are low. Plato mercifully kept the poets out of his. Republics are not congenial soil for poetry."

"What nonsense! If England dropped its fad of Monarchy and became a Republic tomorrow, do you mean to say that...?"

"I mean to say there would be no Poet Laureate to begin with."

"Who's fribbling now, you or me, Cantercot? But I don't care a button-hook about poets, present company always excepted. I'm only a plain man, and I want to know where's the sense of givin' any one person authority over everybody else?"

"Ah, that's what Tom Mortlake used to say. Wait till you're in power, Peter, with trade union money to control, and working men bursting to give you flying angels and to carry you aloft, like a banner, huzzahing."

"Ah, that's because he's head and shoulders above 'em already," said Crowl, with a flash in his sad grey eyes. "Still, it don't prove that I'd talk any different. And I think you're quite wrong about his being spoilt. Tom's a fine fellow - a man every inch of him, and that's a good many. I don't deny he has his weaknesses, and there was a time when he stood in this very shop and denounced that poor dead Constant. 'Crowl,' said he, 'that man'll do mischief. I don't like these kid glove philanthropists mixing themselves up in practical labor disputes they don't understand.'"

Denzil whistled involuntarily. It was a piece of news.

"I dare say," continued Crowl, "he's a bit jealous of anybody's interference with his influence. But in this case the jealousy did wear off, you see, for the poor fellow and he got quite pals, as everybody knows. Tom's not the man to hug a prejudice. However, all that don't prove nothing against Republics. Look at the Czar and the Jews. I'm only a plain man, but I wouldn't live in Russia not for - not for all the leather in it! An Englishman, taxed as he is to keep up his Fad of Monarchy, is at least king in his own castle, whoever bosses it at Windsor. Excuse me a minute, the missus is callin'."

"Excuse *me* a minute. I'm going, and I want to say before I go - I feel it only right you should know at once - that after what has passed today I can never be on the same footing here as in the - shall I say pleasant? Days of yore."

"Oh, no, Cantercot. Don't say that; don't say that!" pleaded the little cobbler.

"Well, shall I say unpleasant, then?"

"No, no, Cantercot. Don't misunderstand me. Mother has been very much put to it lately to rub along. You see she has such a growing family. It grows daily. But never mind her. You pay whenever you've got the money."

Denzil shook his head. "It cannot be. You know when I came here first I rented your top room and boarded myself. Then I learnt to know you. We talked together. Of the Beautiful. And the Useful. I found you had no soul. But you were honest, and I liked you. I went so far as to take my meals with your family. I made myself at home in your back parlor. But the vase has been shattered (I do not refer to that on the mantelpiece) and though the scent of the roses may cling to it still, it can be pieced together nevermore." He shook his hair sadly and shambled out of the shop. Crowl would have gone after him, but Mrs. Crowl was

73

still calling, and ladies must have the precedence in all polite societies.

Cantercot went straight or as straight as his loose gait permitted to 46 Glover Street, and knocked at the door. Grodman's factotum opened it. She was a pock-marked person, with a brick dust complexion and a coquettish manner.

"Oh! Here we are again!" she said vivaciously.

"Don't talk like a clown," Cantercot snapped. "Is Mr. Grodman in?"

"No, you've put him out," growled the gentleman himself, suddenly appearing in his slippers. "Come in. What the devil have you been doing with yourself since the inquest? Drinking again?"

"I've sworn off. Haven't touched a drop since..."

"The murder?"

"Eh?" said Denzil Cantercot, startled. "What do you mean?"

"What I say. Since December 4. I reckon everything from that murder now as they reckon longitude from Greenwich."

"Oh," said Denzil Cantercot.

"Let me see. Nearly a fortnight. What a long time to keep away from Drink - and Me."

"I don't know which is worse," said Denzil, irritated. "You both steal away my brains."

"Indeed?" said Grodman with an amused smile. "Well, it's only petty pilfering, after all. What's put salt on your wounds?"

"The twenty-fourth edition of my book."

"*Whose* book?"

"Well, *your* book. You must be making piles of money out of *Criminals I have Caught.*"

"'Criminals *I* have Caught,'" corrected Grodman. "My dear Denzil, how often am I to point out that *I* went through the experiences that make the backbone

74

of my book, not *you*? In each case *I* cooked the criminal's goose. Any journalist could have supplied the dressing."

"The contrary. The journeymen of journalism would have left the truth naked. You yourself could have done that for there is no man to beat you at cold, lucid, scientific statement. But I idealized the bare facts and lifted them into the realm of poetry and literature. The twenty-fourth edition of the book attests my success."

"Rot! The twenty-fourth edition was all owing to the murder. Did you do that?"

"You take one up so sharply, Mr. Grodman," said Denzil, changing his tone.

"No - I've retired," laughed Grodman.

Denzil did not reprove the ex-detective's flippancy. He even laughed a little.

"Well, give me another fiver, and I'll cry 'quits.' I'm in debt."

"Not a penny. Why haven't you been to see me since the murder? I had to write that letter to the *Pell Mell Press* myself. You might have earned a crown."

"I've had writer's cramp, and couldn't do your last job. I was coming to tell you so on the morning of the..."

"Murder. So you said at the inquest."

"It's true."

"Of course. Weren't you on your oath? It was very zealous of you to get up so early to tell me. In which hand did you have this cramp?"

"Why, in the right of course."

"And you couldn't write with your left?"

"I don't think I could even hold a pen."

"Or any other instrument, mayhap. What had you been doing to bring it on?"

"Writing too much. That is the only possible cause."

75

"Oh! I didn't know. Writing what?"

Denzil hesitated. "An epic poem."

"No wonder you're in debt. Will a sovereign get you out of it?"

"No; it wouldn't be the least use to me."

"Here it is, then."

Denzil took the coin and his hat.

"Aren't you going to earn it, you beggar? Sit down and write something for me."

Denzil got pen and paper, and took his place.

"What do you want me to write?"

"Your Epic Poem."

Denzil started and flushed. But he set to work. Grodman leaned back in his arm-chair and laughed, studying the poet's grave face.

Denzil wrote three lines and paused.

"Can't remember any more? Well, read me the start."

Denzil read:

"Of man's first disobedience and the fruit
Of that forbidden tree whose mortal taste
Brought death into the world--"

"Hold on!" cried Grodman. "What morbid subjects you choose, to be sure!"

"Morbid! Why, Milton chose the same subject!"

"Blow Milton. Take yourself off - you and your epics."

Denzil went. The pockmarked person opened the street door for him.

"When am I to have that new dress, dear?" she whispered coquettishly.

"I have no money, Jane," he said shortly.

"You have a sovereign."

Denzil gave her the sovereign and slammed the door viciously. Grodman overheard their whispers, and

76

laughed silently. His hearing was acute. Jane had first introduced Denzil to his acquaintance about two years ago, when he spoke of getting an amanuensis, and the poet had been doing odd jobs for him ever since. Grodman argued that Jane had her reasons. Without knowing them, he got a hold over both. There was no one, he felt, he could not get a hold over. All men and women have something to conceal, and you have only to pretend to know what it is. Thus Grodman, who was nothing if not scientific.

Denzil Cantercot shambled home thoughtfully, and abstractedly took his place at the Crowl dinner table.

VI

Mrs. Crowl surveyed Denzil Cantercot so stonily and cut him his beef so savagely that he said grace when the dinner was over. Peter fed his metaphysical genius on tomatoes. He was tolerant enough to allow his family to follow their fads; but no savory smells ever tempted him to be false to his vegetable loves. Besides, meat might have reminded him too much of his work. There is nothing like leather, but Bow beefsteaks occasionally come very near it.

After dinner Denzil usually indulged in poetic reverie. But today he did not take his nap. He went out at once to "raise the wind." But there was a dead calm everywhere. In vain he asked for an advance at the office of the *Mile End Mirror,* to which he contributed scathing leaderettes about vestrymen. In vain he trudged to the City and offered to write the *Ham and Eggs Gazette* an essay on the modern methods of bacon curing. Denzil knew a great deal about the breeding and slaughtering of pigs, smoke lofts and drying processes, having for years dictated the policy of the *New Pork Herald* in these momentous matters. Denzil also knew a great deal about many other esoteric matters, including weaving machines, the

79

manufacture of cabbage leaves and snuff, and the inner economy of drain pipes. He had written for the trade papers since boyhood. But there is great competition on these papers. So many men of literary gifts know all about the intricate technicalities of manufactures and markets, and are eager to set the trade right. Grodman perhaps hardly allowed sufficiently for the step backwards that Denzil made when he devoted his whole time for months to *Criminals I have Caught*. It was as damaging as a debauch. For when your rivals are pushing forwards, to stand still is to go back.

In despair Denzil shambled toilsomely to Bethnal Green. He paused before the window of a little tobacconist's shop, wherein was displayed a placard announcing:

PLOTS FOR SALE

The announcement went on to state that a large stock of plots was to be obtained on the premises; embracing sensational plots, humorous plots, love plots, religious plots, and poetic plots; also complete manuscripts, original novels, poems, and tales. Apply within.

It was a very dirty looking shop, with begrimed bricks and blackened woodwork. The window contained some musty old books, an assortment of pipes and tobacco, and a large number of the vilest daubs unhung, painted in oil on Academy boards, and unframed. These were intended for landscapes, as you could tell from the titles. The most expensive was "Chingford Church," and it was marked 1S. 9d. The others ran from 6d. to 1S. 3d., and were mostly representations of Scottish scenery: a loch with mountains in the background, with solid reflections in the water and a tree in the foreground. Sometimes the tree would be in the background. Then the loch would be in the foreground. Sky and water were intensely blue in all. The name of the collection was "Original Oil Paintings Done by Hand." Dust lay thick upon everything, as if carefully shoveled on; and the proprietor looked as if he slept in his shop window at night without taking his clothes off. He was a gaunt man with a red nose, long but scanty black locks covered by a smoking-cap, and a luxuriant black moustache. He smoked a long clay pipe, and had the air of a broken down operatic villain.

"Ah, good afternoon, Mr. Cantercot," he said, rubbing his hands, half from cold, half from usage; "what have you brought me?"

"Nothing," said Denzil, "but if you will lend me a sovereign I'll do you a stunner."

The operatic villain shook his locks, his eyes full of pawky cunning. "If you did it after that, it *would* be a stunner."

What the operatic villain did with these plots, and who bought them, Cantercot never knew nor cared to know. Brains are cheap today, and Denzil was glad enough to find a customer.

"Surely you've known me long enough to trust me," he cried.

"Trust is dead," said the operatic villain, puffing away.

"So is Queen Anne," cried the irritated poet. His eyes took a dangerous hunted look. Money he must have. But the operatic villain was inflexible. No plot, no supper.

Poor Denzil went out flaming. He knew not where to turn. Temporarily he turned on his heel again and stared despairingly at the shop-window. Again he read the legend:

PLOTS FOR SALE

He stared so long at this that it lost its meaning. When the sense of the words suddenly flashed upon him again, they bore a new significance. He went in meekly, and borrowed fourpence of the operatic villain. Then he took the 'bus for Scotland Yard.

There was a not ill-looking servant girl in the 'bus. The rhythm of the vehicle shaped itself into rhymes in his brain. He forgot all about his situation and his object. He had never really written an epic except "Paradise Lost" but he composed lyrics about wine and women and often wept to think how miserable he was. But nobody ever bought anything of him, except articles on bacon curing or attacks on vestrymen. He was a strange, wild creature, and the wench felt quite pretty under his ardent gaze. It almost hypnotized her, though, and she looked down at her new French kid boots to escape it.

At Scotland Yard, Denzil asked for Edward Wimp. Edward Wimp was not on view. Like kings and editors, detectives are difficult of approach unless you are a criminal, when you cannot see anything of them at all. Denzil knew of Edward Wimp, principally because of Grodman's contempt for his successor. Wimp was a man of taste and culture. Grodman's interests were entirely concentrated on the problems of logic and evidence. Books about these formed his sole reading; for *belles lettres* he cared not a straw. Wimp, with his flexible intellect, had a great contempt for Grodman and his slow, laborious, ponderous, almost Teutonic methods. Worse, he almost threatened to eclipse the radiant tradition of Grodman by some wonderfully ingenious bits of workmanship. Wimp was at his greatest in collecting circumstantial evidence; in putting two and two together to make five. He would collect together a number of dark and disconnected data and flash across them the electric light of some unifying hypothesis in a way which would have done credit to a Darwin or a Faraday. An intellect which might have served to unveil the secret workings of nature was subverted to the protection of a capitalistic civilization.

By the assistance of a friendly policeman, whom the poet magnetized into the belief that his business was a matter of life and death, Denzil obtained the great detective's private address. It was near King's Cross. By a miracle, Wimp was at home in the afternoon. He was writing when Denzil was ushered up three pairs of stairs into his presence, but he got up and flashed the bull's-eye of his glance upon the visitor.

"Mr. Denzil Cantercot, I believe," said Wimp.

Denzil started. He had not sent up his name, merely describing himself as a gentleman.

"That is my name," he murmured.

"You were one of the witnesses at the inquest on the body of the late Arthur Constant. I have your evidence there." He pointed to a file. "Why have you come to give fresh evidence?"

Again Denzil started, flushing in addition this time. "I want money," he said, almost involuntarily.

"Sit down."

Denzil sat. Wimp stood.

Wimp was young and fresh-colored. He had a Roman nose, and was smartly dressed. He had beaten Grodman by discovering the wife Heaven meant for him. He had a bouncing boy, who stole jam out of the pantry without anyone being the wiser. Wimp did what work he could do at home in a secluded study at the top of the house. Outside his chamber of horrors, he was the ordinary husband of commerce. He adored his wife, who thought poorly of his intellect but highly of his heart. In domestic difficulties, Wimp was helpless. He could not tell even whether the servant's "character" was forged or genuine. Probably he could not level himself to such petty problems. He was like the senior wrangler who has forgotten how to do quadratics, and has to solve equations of the second degree by the calculus.

"How much money do you want?" he asked.

"I do not make bargains," Denzil replied, his calm come back by this time. "I came here to tender you a suggestion. It struck me that you might offer me a fiver for my trouble. Should you do so, I shall not refuse it."

"You shall not refuse it, if you deserve it."

"Good. I will come to the point at once. My suggestion concerns Tom Mortlake."

Denzil threw out the name as if it were a torpedo. Wimp did not move.

"Tom Mortlake," went on Denzil, looking disappointed, "had a sweetheart." He paused impressively.

Wimp said, "Yes?"

"Where is that sweetheart now?"

"Where, indeed?"

"You know about her disappearance?"

"You have just informed me of it."

"Yes, she is gone without a trace. She went about a fortnight before Mr. Constant's murder."

"Murder? How do you know it was murder?"

"Mr. Grodman says so," said Denzil, startled again.

"H'm! Isn't that rather a proof that it was suicide? Well, go on."

"About a fortnight before the suicide, Jessie Dymond disappeared. So they tell me in Stepney Green, where she lodged and worked."

"What was she?"

"She was a dressmaker. She had a wonderful talent. Quite fashionable ladies got to know of it. One of her dresses was presented at Court. I think the lady forgot to pay for it; so Jessie's landlady said."

"Did she live alone?"

"She had no parents, but the house was respectable."

"Good looking, I suppose?"

"As a poet's dream."

"As yours, for instance?"

"I am a poet; I dream."

"You dream you are a poet. Well, well! She was engaged to Mortlake?"

"Oh, yes! They made no secret of it. The engagement was an old one. When he was earning 36s a week as a compositor, they were saving up to buy a home. He worked at Railton and Hockes who print the *New Pork Herald*. I used to take my 'copy' into the comps' room, and one day the Father of the Chapel told me all about 'Mortlake and his young woman.' Ye gods! How times are changed! Two years ago Mortlake had to struggle with my calligraphy. Now he is in with all the nobs, and goes to the 'At Homes' of the aristocracy."

"Radical M.P.'s," murmured Wimp, smiling.

"While I am still barred from the dazzling drawing rooms, where beauty and intellect foregather. A mere artisan! A manual laborer!" Denzil's eyes flashed angrily. He rose with excitement. "They say he always *was* a jabberer in the composing room, and he has jabbered himself right out of it and into a pretty good thing. He didn't have much to say about the crimes of capital when he was set up to second the toast of 'Railton and Hockes' at the beanfeast."

"Toast and butter, toast and butter," said Wimp, genially. "I shouldn't blame a man for serving the two together, Mr. Cantercot."

Denzil forced a laugh. "Yes; but consistency's *my* motto. I like to see the royal soul immaculate, unchanging, immovable by fortune. Anyhow, when better times came for Mortlake the engagement still

86

dragged on. He did not visit her so much. This last autumn he saw very little of her."

"How do you know?"

"I - I was often in Stepney Green. My business took me past the house of an evening. Sometimes there was no light in her room. That meant she was downstairs gossiping with the landlady."

"She might have been out with Tom?"

"No, sir; I knew Tom was on the platform somewhere or other. He was working up to all hours organizing the eight hours' working movement."

"A very good reason for relaxing his sweethearting."

"It was. He never went to Stepney Green on a week night."

"But you always did."

"No. Not every night."

"You didn't go in?"

"Never. She wouldn't permit my visits. She was a girl of strong character. She always reminded me of Flora Macdonald."

"Another lady of your acquaintance?"

"A lady I know better than the shadows who surround me, who is more real to me than the women who pester me for the price of apartments. Jessie Dymond, too, was of the race of heroines. Her eyes were clear blue, two wells with Truth at the bottom of each. When I looked into those eyes my own were dazzled. They were the only eyes I could never make dreamy." He waved his hand as if making a pass with it. "It was she who had the influence over me."

"You knew her, then?"

"Oh, yes. I knew Tom from the old *New Pork Herald* days, and when I first met him with Jessie hanging on his arm he was quite proud to introduce her to a poet. When he got on he tried to shake me off."

"You should have repaid him what you borrowed."

"It – it - was only a trifle," stammered Denzil.

"Yes, but the world turns on trifles," said the wise Wimp.

"The world is itself a trifle," said the pensive poet. "The Beautiful alone is deserving of our regard."

"And when the Beautiful was not gossiping with her landlady, did she gossip with you as you passed the door?"

"Alas, no! She sat in her room reading, and cast a shadow..."

"On your life?"

"No; on the blind."

"Always one shadow?"

"No, sir. Once or twice, two."

"Ah, you had been drinking."

"On my life, not. I have sworn off the treacherous wine cup."

"That's right. Beer is bad for poets. It makes their feet shaky. Whose was the second shadow?"

"A man's."

"Naturally. Mortlake's, perhaps."

"Impossible. He was still striking eight hours."

"You found out whose shadow? You didn't leave a shadow of doubt?"

"No; I waited till the substance came out."

"It was Arthur Constant."

"You are a magician! You - you terrify me. Yes, it was he."

"Only once or twice, you say?"

"I didn't keep watch over them."

"No, no, of course not. You only passed casually. I understand you thoroughly."

Denzil did not feel comfortable at the assertion.

"What did he go there for?" Wimp went on.

"I don't know. I'd stake my soul on Jessie's honor."

"You might double your stake without risk."

"Yes, I might! I would! You see her with my eyes."

"For the moment they are the only ones available. When was the last time you saw the two together?"

"About the middle of November."

"Mortlake knew nothing of the meetings?"

"I don't know. Perhaps he did. Mr. Constant had probably enlisted her in his social mission work. I knew she was one of the attendants at the big children's tea in the Great Assembly Hall early in November. He treated her quite like a lady. She was the only attendant who worked with her hands."

"The others carried the cups on their feet, I suppose."

"No; how could that be? My meaning is that all the other attendants were real ladies, and Jessie was only an amateur, so to speak. There was no novelty for her in handing kids cups of tea. I dare say she had helped her landlady often enough at that. There's quite a bushel of brats below stairs. It's almost as bad as at friend Crowl's. Jessie was a real brick. But perhaps Tom didn't know her value. Perhaps he didn't like Constant to call on her, and it led to a quarrel. Anyhow, she's disappeared, like the snowfall on the river. There's not a trace. The landlady, who was such a friend of hers that Jessie used to make up her stuff into dresses for nothing, tells me that she's dreadfully annoyed at not having been left the slightest clue to her late tenant's whereabouts."

"You have been making inquiries on your own account apparently?"

"Only of the landlady. Jessie never even gave her the week's notice, but paid her in lieu of it, and left immediately. The landlady told me I could have knocked her down with a feather. Unfortunately, I wasn't there to do it, or I should certainly have knocked her down for not keeping her eyes open better. She says if she had only had the least suspicion beforehand that the minx (she dared to call Jessie a minx) was going, she'd have known where, or her name would have been somebody else's. And yet she admits that Jessie was looking ill and worried. Stupid old hag!"

"A woman of character," murmured the detective.

"Didn't I tell you so?" cried Denzil, eagerly. "Another girl would have let out that she was going. But no, not a word. She plumped down the money and walked out. The landlady ran upstairs. None of Jessie's things were there. She must have quietly sold them off, or transferred them to the new place. I never in my life met a girl who so thoroughly knew her own mind or had a mind so worth knowing. She always reminded me of the Maid of Saragossa."

"Indeed! And when did she leave?"

"On the 19th of November."

"Mortlake of course knows where she is?"

"I can't say. Last time I was at the house to inquire - it was at the end of November - he hadn't been seen there for six weeks. He wrote to her, of course, sometimes; the landlady knew his writing."

Wimp looked Denzil straight in the eyes, and said, "You mean, of course, to accuse Mortlake of the murder of Mr. Constant?"

"N-n-no, not at all," stammered Denzil, "only you know what Mr. Grodman wrote to the *Pell Mell*. The more we know about Mr. Constant's life the more we shall know about the manner of his death. I thought my information would be valuable to you, and I brought it."

"And why didn't you take it to Mr. Grodman?"

"Because I thought it wouldn't be valuable to *me*."

"You wrote *Criminals I have Caught?*"

"How - how do you know that?" Wimp was startling him today with a vengeance.

"Your style, my dear Mr. Cantercot. The unique, noble style."

"Yes, I was afraid it would betray me," said Denzil. "And since you know, I may tell you that Grodman's a mean curmudgeon. What does he want with all that money and those houses; a man with no sense of the Beautiful? He'd have taken my information, and given me more kicks than ha'pence for it, so to speak."

"Yes, he is a shrewd man after all. I don't see anything valuable in your evidence against Mortlake."

"No!" said Denzil in a disappointed tone, and fearing he was going to be robbed. "Not when Mortlake was already jealous of Mr. Constant, who was a sort of rival organizer, unpaid! A kind of blackleg doing the work cheaper - nay, for nothing."

"Did Mortlake tell you he was jealous?" said Wimp, a shade of sarcastic contempt piercing through his tones.

"Oh, yes! He said to me, 'That man will work mischief. I don't like your kid glove philanthropists meddling in matters they don't understand.'"

"Those were his very words?"

"His *ipsissima verba.*"

"Very well. I have your address in my files. Here is a sovereign for you."

"Only one sovereign! It's not the least use to me."

"Very well. It's of great use to me. I have a wife to keep."

"I haven't," said Denzil, with a sickly smile, "so perhaps I can manage on it after all." He took his hat and the sovereign.

Outside the door he met a rather pretty servant just bringing in some tea to her master. He nearly upset her tray at sight of her. She seemed more amused at the *rencontre* than he.

"Good afternoon, dear," she said coquettishly. "You might let me have that sovereign. I do so want a new Sunday bonnet."

Denzil gave her the sovereign, and slammed the hall door viciously when he got to the bottom of the stairs. He seemed to be walking arm-in-arm with the long arm of coincidence. Wimp did not hear the duologue. He was already busy on his evening's report to headquarters. The next day Denzil had a bodyguard wherever he went. It might have gratified his vanity had he known it. But tonight he was yet unattended, so no one noted that he went to 46 Glover Street, after the early Crowl supper. He could not help going. He wanted to get another sovereign. He also itched to taunt Grodman. Not succeeding in the former object, he felt the road open for the second.

"Do you still hope to discover the Bow murderer?" he asked the old bloodhound.

"I can lay my hand on him now," Grodman announced curtly.

Denzil hitched his chair back involuntarily. He found conversation with detectives as lively as playing at skittles with bombshells. They got on his nerves terribly, these undemonstrative gentlemen with no sense of the Beautiful.

"But why don't you give him up to justice?" he murmured.

"Ah - it has to be proved yet. But it is only a matter of time."

"Oh!" said Denzil, "and shall I write the story for you?"

"No. You will not live long enough."

Denzil turned white. "Nonsense! I am years younger than you," he gasped.

"Yes," said Grodman, "but you drink so much."

VII

When Wimp invited Grodman to eat his
Christmas plum pudding at King's Cross, Grodman
was only a little surprised. The two men were always
overwhelmingly cordial when they met, in order to
disguise their mutual detestation. When people really
like each other, they make no concealment of their
mutual contempt. In his letter to Grodman, Wimp said
that he thought it might be nicer for him to keep
Christmas in company than in solitary state. There
seems to be a general prejudice in favor of Christmas
numbers, and Grodman yielded to it. Besides, he
thought that a peep at the Wimp domestic interior
would be as good as a pantomime. He quite enjoyed
the fun that was coming, for he knew that Wimp had
not invited him out of mere "peace and goodwill."

There was only one other guest at the festive
board. This was Wimp's wife's mother's mother, a lady
of sweet seventy. Only a minority of mankind can
obtain a grandmother-in-law by marrying, but Wimp
was not unduly conceited. The old lady suffered from
delusions. One of them was that she was a
centenarian. She dressed for the part. It is
extraordinary what pains ladies will take to conceal

their age. Another of Wimp's grandmother-in-law's delusions was that Wimp had married to get her into the family. Not to frustrate his design, she always gave him her company on high days and holidays. Wilfred Wimp - the little boy who stole the jam - was in great form at the Christmas dinner. The only drawback to his enjoyment was that its sweets needed no stealing. His mother presided over the platters, and thought how much cleverer Grodman was than her husband. When the pretty servant who waited on them was momentarily out of the room, Grodman had remarked that she seemed very inquisitive. This coincided with Mrs. Wimp's own convictions, though Mr. Wimp could never be brought to see anything unsatisfactory or suspicious about the girl, not even though there were faults in spelling in the "character" with which her last mistress had supplied her.

It was true that the puss had pricked up her ears when Denzil Cantercot's name was mentioned. Grodman saw it, and watched her, and fooled Wimp to the top of his bent. It was, of course, Wimp who introduced the poet's name, and he did it so casually that Grodman perceived at once that he wished to pump him. The idea that the rival bloodhound should come to him for confirmation of suspicions against his own pet jackal was too funny. It was almost as funny to Grodman that evidence of some sort should be obviously lying to hand in the bosom of Wimp's handmaiden; so obviously that Wimp could not see it. Grodman enjoyed his Christmas dinner, secure that he had not found a successor after all. Wimp, for his part, contemptuously wondered at the way Grodman's thought hovered about Denzil without grazing the truth. A man constantly about him, too!

"Denzil is a man of genius," said Grodman. "And as such comes under the heading of Suspicious Characters. He has written an Epic Poem and read it to me. It is morbid from start to finish. There is 'death' in the third line. I dare say you know he polished up my book?" Grodman's artlessness was perfect.

"No. You surprise me," Wimp replied. "I'm sure he couldn't have done much to it. Look at your letter in the Pell Mell. Who wants more polish and refinement than that showed?"

"Ah, I didn't know you did me the honor of reading that."

"Oh, yes; we both read it," put in Mrs. Wimp. "I told Mr. Wimp it was very clever and cogent. After that quotation from the letter to the poor fellow's *fiancée* there could be no more doubt but that it was murder. Mr. Wimp was convinced by it too, weren't you, Edward?"

Edward coughed uneasily. It was a true statement, and therefore indiscreet. Grodman would plume himself terribly. At this moment Wimp felt that Grodman had been right in remaining a bachelor. Grodman perceived the humor of the situation and wore a curious, sub-mocking smile.

"On the day I was born," said Wimp's grandmother-in-law, "over a hundred years ago, there was a babe murdered." Wimp found himself wishing it had been she. He was anxious to get back to Cantercot. "Don't let us talk shop on Christmas Day," he said smiling at Grodman. "Besides, murder isn't a very appropriate subject."

"No, it ain't," said Grodman. "How did we get on to it? Oh, yes - Denzil Cantercot. Ha! Ha! Ha! That's curious, for since Denzil revised *Criminals I have Caught,* his mind's running on nothing but murders. A poet's brain is easily turned."

Wimp's eye glittered with excitement and contempt for Grodman's blindness. In Grodman's eye there danced an amused scorn of Wimp; to the outsider his amusement appeared at the expense of the poet.

Having wrought his rival up to the highest pitch, Grodman slyly and suddenly unstrung him.

"How lucky for Denzil!" he said, still in the same naive, facetious Christmasy tone, "that he can prove an alibi in this Constant affair."

"An alibi!" gasped Wimp. "Really?"

"Oh, yes. He was with his wife, you know. She's my woman of all work, Jane. She happened to mention his being with her."

Jane had done nothing of the kind. After the colloquy he had overheard, Grodman had set himself to find out the relation between his two employees. By casually referring to Denzil as "your husband," he so startled the poor woman that she did not attempt to deny the bond. Only once did he use the two words, but he was satisfied. As to the alibi, he had not yet troubled her; but to take its existence for granted would upset and discomfort Wimp. For the moment that was triumph enough for Wimp's guest.

"Par," said Wilfred Wimp, "what's a alleybi? A marble?"

"No, my lad," said Grodman, "it means being somewhere else when you're supposed to be somewhere."

"Ah, playing truant," said Wilfred, self-consciously; his schoolmaster had often proved an alibi against him. "Then Denzil will be hanged."

Was it a prophecy? Wimp accepted it as such; as an oracle from the gods bidding him mistrust Grodman. Out of the mouths of little children issueth wisdom; sometimes even when they are not saying their lessons.

"When I was in my cradle, a century ago," said Wimp's grandmother-in-law, "men were hanged for stealing horses."

They silenced her with snapdragon performances.

Wimp was busy thinking how to get at Grodman's factotum.

Grodman was busy thinking how to get at Wimp's domestic.

Neither received any of the usual messages from the Christmas Bells.

The next day was sloppy and uncertain. A thin rain drizzled languidly. One can stand that sort of thing on a summer Bank Holiday; one expects it. But to have a bad December Bank Holiday is too much of a bad thing. Some steps should surely be taken to confuse the weather clerk's chronology. Once let him know that Bank Holiday is coming, and he writes to the company for more water. Today his stock seemed low, and he was dribbling it out; at times the wintry sun would shine in a feeble, diluted way, and though the holiday-makers would have preferred to take their sunshine neat, they swarmed forth in their myriads whenever there was a ray of hope. But it was only dodging the raindrops; up went the umbrellas again, and the streets became meadows of ambulating mushrooms.

Denzil Cantercot sat in his fur overcoat at the open window, looking at the landscape in watercolors. He smoked an after dinner cigarette, and spoke of the Beautiful. Crowl was with him. They were in the first floor front, Crowl's bedroom, which, from its view of the Mile End Road, was livelier than the parlor with its outlook on the backyard. Mrs. Crowl was an anti-tobacconist as regards the best bedroom; but Peter did not like to put the poet or his cigarette out. He felt there was something in common between smoke and poetry, over and above their being both Fads. Besides, Mrs. Crowl was sulking in the kitchen. She had been arranging for an excursion with Peter and the children to Victoria Park. (She had dreamed of the Crystal Palace, but Santa Claus had put no gifts in the cobbler's shoes.) Now she could not risk spoiling the feather in her bonnet. The nine brats expressed their disappointment by slapping one another on the staircases. Peter felt that Mrs. Crowl connected him in some way with the rainfall, and was unhappy. Was it not enough that he had been deprived of the pleasure of pointing out to a superstitious majority the mutual contradictions of Leviticus and the Song of Solomon? It was not often that Crowl could count on such an audience.

"And you still call Nature Beautiful?" he said to Denzil, pointing to the ragged sky and the dripping eaves. "Ugly old scarecrow!"

"Ugly she seems today," admitted Denzil. "But what is Ugliness but a higher form of Beauty? You have to look deeper into it to see it; such vision is the priceless gift of the few. To me this wan desolation of sighing rain is lovely as the sea-washed ruins of cities."

"Ah, but you wouldn't like to go out into it," said Peter Crowl. As he spoke the drizzle suddenly thickened into a torrent.

"We do not always kiss the woman we love."

"Speak for yourself, Denzil. I'm only a plain man, and I want to know if Nature isn't a Fad. Hallo, there goes Mortlake! Lord, a minute of this will soak him to the skin."

The labor leader was walking along with bowed head. He did not seem to mind the shower. It was some seconds before he even heard Crowl's invitation to him to take shelter. When he did hear it he shook his head.

"I know I can't offer you a drawing room with duchesses stuck about it," said Peter, vexed.

Tom turned the handle of the shop door and went in. There was nothing in the world which now galled him more than the suspicion that he was stuck up and wished to cut old friends. He picked his way through the nine brats who clung affectionately to his wet knees, dispersing them finally by a jet of coppers to scramble for. Peter met him on the stairs and shook his hand lovingly and admiringly, and took him into Mrs. Crowl's bedroom.

"Don't mind what I say, Tom. I'm only a plain man, and my tongue will say what comes uppermost! But it ain't from the soul, Tom, it ain't from the soul," said Peter, punning feebly, and letting a mirthless smile play over his sallow features. "You know Mr. Cantercot, I suppose? The Poet."

"Oh, yes; how do you do, Tom?" cried the Poet. "Seen the *New Pork Herald* lately? Not bad, those old times, eh?"

"No," said Tom, "I wish I was back in them."

"Nonsense, nonsense," said Peter, in much concern. "Look at the good you are doing to the working man. Look how you are sweeping away the Fads. Ah, it's a grand thing to be gifted, Tom. The idea of your chuckin' yourself away on a composin'-room! Manual labor is all very well for plain men like me, with no gift but just enough brains to see into the realities of things - to understand that we've got no soul and no immortality, and all that - and too selfish to look after anybody's comfort but my own and mother's and the kids'. But men like you and Cantercot - it ain't right that you should be peggin' away at low material things. Not that I think Cantercot's gospel any value to the masses. The Beautiful is all very well for folks who've got nothing else to think of, but give me the True. You're the man for my money, Mortlake. No reference to the funds, Tom, to which I contribute little enough, Heaven knows; though how a *place* can know anything, Heaven alone knows. *You* give us the Useful, Tom; that's what the world wants more than the Beautiful."

"Socrates said that the Useful *is* the Beautiful," said Denzil.

"That may be," said Peter, "but the Beautiful ain't the Useful."

"Nonsense!" said Denzil. "What about Jessie - I mean Miss Dymond? There's a combination for you. She always reminds me of Grace Darling. How *is* she, Tom?"

"She's dead!" snapped Tom.

"What?" Denzil turned as white as a Christmas ghost.

"It was in the papers," said Tom; "all about her and the lifeboat."

"Oh, you mean Grace Darling," said Denzil, visibly relieved. "I meant Miss Dymond."

"You needn't be so interested in her," said Tom surlily. "She don't appreciate it. Ah, the shower is over. I must be going."

"No, stay a little longer, Tom," pleaded Peter.

"I see a lot about you in the papers, but very little of your dear old phiz now. I can't spare the time to go and hear you. But I really must give myself a treat. When's your next show?"

"Oh, I am always giving shows," said Tom, smiling a little. "But my next big performance is on the twenty-first of January, when that picture of poor Mr. Constant is to be unveiled at the Bow Break o' Day Club. They have written to Gladstone and other big pots to come down. I do hope the old man accepts. A non-political gathering like this is the only occasion we could both speak at, and I have never been on the same platform with Gladstone."

He forgot his depression and ill-temper in the prospect, and spoke with more animation.

"No, I should hope not, Tom," said Peter. "What with his Fads about the Bible being a Rock, and Monarchy being the right thing, he is a most dangerous man to lead the Radicals. He never lays his axe to the root of anything - except oak trees."

"Mr. Cantycot!" It was Mrs. Crowl's voice that broke in upon the tirade. "There's a *gentleman* to see you." The astonishment Mrs. Crowl put into the "gentleman" was delightful. It was almost as good as a week's rent to her to give vent to her feelings. The controversial couple had moved away from the window when Tom entered, and had not noticed the immediate advent of another visitor who had spent his time profitably in listening to Mrs. Crowl before asking to see the presumable object of his visit.

"Ask him up if it's a friend of yours, Cantercot," said Peter. It was Wimp. Denzil was rather dubious as to the friendship, but he preferred to take Wimp diluted. "Mortlake's upstairs," he said; "will you come up and see him?"

Wimp had intended a duologue, but he made no objection, so he, too, stumbled through the nine brats to Mrs. Crowl's bedroom. It was a queer quartette. Wimp had hardly expected to find anybody at the house on Boxing Day, but he did not care to waste a day. Was not Grodman, too, on the track? How lucky it was that Denzil had made the first overtures, so that he could approach him without exciting suspicion.

Mortlake scowled when he saw the detective. He objected to the police on principle. But Crowl had no idea who the visitor was, even when told his name. He was rather pleased to meet one of Denzil's high class friends, and welcomed him warmly. Probably he was some famous editor, which would account for his name stirring vague recollections. He summoned the eldest brat and sent him for beer (people would have their Fads), and not without trepidation called down to

"Mother" for glasses. "Mother" observed at night (in the same apartment) that the beer money might have paid the week's school fees for half the family.

"We were just talking of poor Mr. Constant's portrait, Mr. Wimp," said the unconscious Crowl; "they're going to unveil it, Mortlake tells me, on the twenty-first of next month at the Bow Break o' Day Club."

"Ah," said Wimp, elate at being spared the trouble of maneuvering the conversation; "mysterious affair that, Mr. Crowl."

"No; it's the right thing," said Peter. "There ought to be some memorial of the man in the district where he worked and where he died, poor chap." The cobbler brushed away a tear.

"Yes, it's only right," echoed Mortlake, a whit eagerly. "He was a noble fellow, a true philanthropist - the only thoroughly unselfish worker I've ever met."

"He was that," said Peter; "and it's a rare pattern is unselfishness. Poor fellow, poor fellow. He preached the Useful, too. I've never met his like. Ah, I wish there was a heaven for him to go to!" He blew his nose violently with a red pocket handkerchief.

"Well, he's there, if there *is*," said Tom.

"I hope he is," added Wimp, fervently; "but I shouldn't like to go there the way he did."

"You were the last person to see him, Tom, weren't you?" said Denzil.

"Oh, no," answered Tom, quickly. "You remember he went out after me; at least, so Mrs. Drabdump said at the inquest."

"That last conversation he had with you, Tom," said Denzil. "He didn't say anything to you that would lead you to suppose..."

"No, of course not!" interrupted Mortlake, impatiently.

"Do you really think he was murdered, Tom?" said Denzil.

"Mr. Wimp's opinion on that point is more valuable than mine," replied Tom, testily. "It may have been suicide. Men often get sick of life, especially if they are bored," he added meaningly.

"Ah, but you were the last person known to be with him," said Denzil.

Crowl laughed. "Had you there, Tom."

But they did not have Tom there much longer, for he departed, looking even worse-tempered than when he came. Wimp went soon after, and Crowl and Denzil were left to their interminable argumentation concerning the Useful and the Beautiful.

Wimp went West. He had several strings (or cords) to his bow, and he ultimately found himself at Kensal Green Cemetery. Being there, he went down the avenues of the dead to a grave to note down the exact date of a death. It was a day on which the dead seemed enviable. The dull, sodden sky, the dripping, leafless trees, the wet, spongy soil, the reeking grass - everything combined to make one long to be in a warm, comfortable grave away from the leaden *ennui* of life. Suddenly the detective's keen eye caught sight of a figure that made his heart throb with sudden excitement. It was that of a woman in a grey shawl and a brown bonnet, standing before a railed-in grave. She had no umbrella. The rain plashed mournfully upon her, but left no trace on her soaking garments. Wimp crept up behind her, but she paid no heed to him. Her eyes were lowered to the grave, which seemed to be drawing them towards it by some strange morbid fascination. His eyes followed hers. The simple headstone bore the name, "Arthur Constant."

Wimp tapped her suddenly on the shoulder.

"How do you do, Mrs. Drabdump?"

Mrs. Drabdump went deadly white. She turned round, staring at Wimp without any recognition.

"You remember me, surely," he said; "I've been down once or twice to your place about that poor gentleman's papers." His eye indicated the grave.

"Lor! I remember you now," said Mrs. Drabdump.

"Won't you come under my umbrella? You must be drenched to the skin."

"It don't matter, sir. I can't take no hurt. I've had the rheumatics this twenty year."

Mrs. Drabdump shrank from accepting Wimp's attentions, not so much perhaps because he was a man as because he was a gentleman. Mrs. Drabdump liked to see the fine folks keep their place, and not contaminate their skirts by contact with the lower castes. "It's set wet, it'll rain right into the new year," she announced. "And they say a bad beginnin' makes a worse endin'." Mrs. Drabdump was one of those persons who give you the idea that they just missed being born barometers.

"But what are you doing in this miserable spot, so far from home?" queried the detective.

"It's Bank Holiday," Mrs. Drabdump reminded him in tones of acute surprise. "I always make a hexcursion on Bank Holiday."

VIII

The New Year drew Mrs. Drabdump a new lodger. He was an old gentleman with a long grey beard. He rented the rooms of the late Mr. Constant, and lived a very retired life. Haunted rooms - or rooms that ought to be haunted if the ghosts of those murdered in them had any self-respect - are supposed to fetch a lower rent in the market. The whole Irish problem might be solved if the spirits of "Mr. Balfour's victims" would only depreciate the value of property to a point consistent with the support of an agricultural population. But Mrs. Drabdump's new lodger paid so much for his rooms that he laid himself open to a suspicion of a special interest in ghosts. Perhaps he was a member of the Psychical Society. The neighborhood imagined him another mad philanthropist, but as he did not appear to be doing any good to anybody it relented and conceded his sanity. Mortlake, who occasionally stumbled across him in the passage, did not trouble himself to think about him at all. He was too full of other troubles and cares. Though he worked harder than ever, the spirit seemed to have gone out of him. Sometimes he forgot himself in a fine rapture of eloquence – lashing himself up into a divine resentment of injustice or a passion of sympathy with the sufferings of his brethren - but mostly he plodded on in dull, mechanical fashion. He still made brief provincial tours, starring a day here and a day there, and everywhere his admirers remarked how jaded and overworked he looked. There was talk of starting a subscription to give him a holiday on the Continent - a luxury obviously unobtainable on the few pounds allowed him per week. The new lodger would doubtless have been pleased to subscribe, for he seemed quite to like occupying Mortlake's chamber the nights he was absent, though he was thoughtful enough not to disturb the hard worked landlady in the adjoining room by unseemly noise. Wimp was always a quiet man.

Meantime the twenty-first of the month approached, and the East End was in excitement. Mr. Gladstone had consented to be present at the ceremony of unveiling the portrait of Arthur Constant, presented by an unknown donor to the Bow Break o' Day Club, and it was to be a great function. The whole affair was outside the lines of party politics, so that even Conservatives and Socialists considered themselves justified in pestering the committee for tickets. To say nothing of ladies! As the committee desired to be present themselves, nine-tenths of the applications for admission had to be refused, as is usual on these occasions. The committee agreed among themselves to exclude the fair sex altogether as the only way of disposing of their womankind, who were making speeches as long as Mr. Gladstone's. Each committeeman told his sisters, female cousins, and aunts, that the other committeemen had insisted on divesting the function of all grace; and what could a man do when he was in a minority of one?

Crowl, who was not a member of the Break o' Day Club, was particularly anxious to hear the great orator whom he despised; fortunately Mortlake remembered the cobbler's anxiety to hear himself, and on the eve of the ceremony sent him a ticket. Crowl was in the first flush of possession when Denzil Cantercot returned, after a sudden and unannounced absence of three days. His clothes were muddy and tattered, his cocked hat was deformed, his cavalier beard was matted, and his eyes were bloodshot. The cobbler nearly dropped the ticket at the sight of him. "Hallo, Cantercot!" he gasped. "Why, where have you been all these days?"

"Terribly busy!" said Denzil. "Here, give me a glass of water. I'm dry as the Sahara."

Crowl ran inside and got the water, trying hard not to inform Mrs. Crowl of their lodger's return. "Mother" had expressed herself freely on the subject of the poet during his absence, and not in terms which would have commended themselves to the poet's fastidious literary sense. Indeed, she did not hesitate to call him a sponger and a low swindler, who had run away to avoid paying the piper. Her fool of a husband might be quite sure he would never set eyes on the scoundrel again. However, Mrs. Crowl was wrong. Here was Denzil back again. And yet Mr. Crowl felt no sense of victory. He had no desire to crow over his partner and to utter that "See! Didn't I tell you so?" which is a greater consolation than religion in most of the misfortunes of life. Unfortunately, to get the water, Crowl had to go to the kitchen; and as he was usually such a temperate man, this desire for drink in the middle of the day attracted the attention of the lady in possession. Crowl had to explain the situation. Mrs. Crowl ran into the shop to improve it. Mr. Crowl followed in dismay, leaving a trail of spilt water in his wake.

"You good-for-nothing, disreputable scarecrow, where have..."

"Hush, mother. Let him drink. Mr. Cantercot is thirsty."

"Does he care if my children are hungry?"

Denzil tossed the water greedily down his throat almost at a gulp, as if it were brandy.

"Madam," he said, smacking his lips, "I do care. I care intensely. Few things in life would grieve me more deeply than to hear that a child, a dear little child - the Beautiful in a nutshell - had suffered hunger. You wrong me." His voice was tremulous with the sense of injury. Tears stood in his eyes.

"Wrong you? I've no wish to *wrong* you," said Mrs. Crowl. "I should like to *hang* you."

"Don't talk of such ugly things," said Denzil, touching his throat nervously.

"Well, what have you been doin' all this time?"

"Why, what should I be doing?"

"How should I know what became of you? I thought it was another murder."

"What!" Denzil's glass dashed to fragments on the floor. "What do you mean?"

But Mrs. Crowl was glaring too viciously at Mr. Crowl to reply. He understood the message as if it were printed. It ran: "You have broken one of my best glasses. You have annihilated threepence, or a week's school fees for half the family." Peter wished she would turn the lightning upon Denzil, a conductor down whom it would run innocuously. He stooped down and picked up the pieces as carefully as if they were cuttings from the Koh-i-noor. Thus the lightning passed harmlessly over his head and flew towards Cantercot.

"What do I mean?" Mrs. Crowl echoed, as if there had been no interval. "I mean that it would be a good thing if you *had* been murdered."

"What unbeautiful ideas you have to be sure!" murmured Denzil.

"Yes; but they'd be useful," said Mrs. Crowl, who had not lived with Peter all these years for nothing. "And if you haven't been murdered, what *have* you been doing?"

"My dear, my dear," put in Crowl, deprecatingly, looking up from his quadrupedal position like a sad dog, "you are not Cantercot's keeper."

"Oh, ain't I?" flashed his spouse. "Who else keeps him, I should like to know?"

Peter went on picking up the pieces of the Koh-i-noor.

"I have no secrets from Mrs. Crowl," Denzil explained courteously. "I have been working day and night bringing out a new paper. Haven't had a wink of sleep for three nights."

Peter looked up at his bloodshot eyes with respectful interest.

"The capitalist met me in the street - an old friend of mine - I was overjoyed at the *rencontre* and told him the idea I'd been brooding over for months, and he promised to stand all the racket."

"What sort of a paper?" said Peter.

"Can you ask? To what do you think I've been devoting my days and nights but to the cultivation of the Beautiful?"

"Is that what the paper will be devoted to?"

"Yes. To the Beautiful."

"I know," snorted Mrs. Crowl, "with portraits of actresses."

"Portraits? Oh no!" said Denzil. "That would be the True, not the Beautiful."

"And what's the name of the paper?" asked Crowl.

"Ah, that's a secret, Peter. Like Scott, I prefer to remain anonymous."

"Just like your Fads. I'm only a plain man, and I want to know where the fun of anonymity comes in. If I had any gifts, I should like to get the credit. It's a right and natural feeling to my thinking."

"Unnatural, Peter; unnatural. We're all born anonymous, and I'm for sticking close to Nature. Enough for me that I disseminate the Beautiful. Any letters come during my absence, Mrs. Crowl?"

"No," she snapped. "But a gent named Grodman called. He said you hadn't been to see him for some time, and looked annoyed to hear you'd disappeared. How much have you let *him* in for?"

"The man's in *my* debt," said Denzil, annoyed. "I wrote a book for him and he's taken all the credit for it, the rogue! My name doesn't appear even in the Preface. What's that ticket you're looking so lovingly at, Peter?"

"That's for tonight; the unveiling of Constant's portrait. Gladstone speaks. Awful demand for places."

"Gladstone!" sneered Denzil. "Who wants to hear Gladstone? A man who's devoted his life to pulling down the pillars of Church and State."

"A man who's devoted his whole life to propping up the crumbling Fads of Religion and Monarchy. But, for all that, the man has his gifts, and I'm burnin' to hear him."

"I wouldn't go out of my way an inch to hear him," said Denzil; and went up to his room, and when Mrs. Crowl sent him up a cup of nice strong tea at tea time, the brat who bore it found him lying dressed on the bed, snoring unbeautifully.

The evening wore on. It was fine frosty weather. The Whitechapel Road swarmed with noisy life, as though it were a Saturday night. The stars flared in the sky like the lights of celestial costermongers. Everybody was on the alert for the advent of Mr. Gladstone. He must surely come through the Road on his journey from the West Bow-wards. But nobody saw him or his carriage, except those about the Hall.

Probably he went by tram most of the way. He would have caught cold in an open carriage, or bobbing his head out of the window of a closed.

"If he had only been a German prince, or a cannibal king," said Crowl, bitterly, as he plodded towards the Club, "we should have disguised Mile End in bunting and blue fire. But perhaps it's a compliment. He knows his London, and it's no use trying to hide the facts from him. They must have queer notions of cities, those monarchs. They must fancy everybody lives in a flutter of flags and walks about under triumphal arches, like as if I were to stitch shoes in my Sunday clothes." By a defiance of chronology Crowl had them on today, and they seemed to accentuate the simile.

"And why shouldn't life be fuller of the Beautiful?" said Denzil. The poet had brushed the reluctant mud off his garments to the extent it was willing to go, and had washed his face, but his eyes were still bloodshot from the cultivation of the Beautiful. Denzil was accompanying Crowl to the door of the Club out of good fellowship. Denzil was himself accompanied by Grodman, though less obtrusively. Least obtrusively was he accompanied by his usual Scotland Yard shadows, Wimp's agents. There was a surging nondescript crowd about the Club, so that the police and the doorkeeper and the stewards could, with difficulty, keep out the tide of the ticketless, through which the current of the privileged had equal difficulty in permeating. The streets all around were thronged with people longing for a glimpse of Gladstone. Mortlake drove up in a hansom (his head a self-conscious pendulum of popularity, swaying and bowing to right and left) and received all the pent-up enthusiasm.

"Well, goodbye, Cantercot," said Crowl.

"No, I'll see you to the door, Peter."

They fought their way shoulder to shoulder.

Now that Grodman had found Denzil he was not going to lose him again. He had only found him by accident, for he was himself bound to the unveiling ceremony, to which he had been invited in view of his known devotion to the task of unveiling the Mystery. He spoke to one of the policemen about, who said, "Ay, ay, sir," and he was prepared to follow Denzil, if necessary, and to give up the pleasure of hearing Gladstone for an acuter thrill. The arrest must be delayed no longer.

But Denzil seemed as if he were going in on the heels of Crowl. This would suit Grodman better. He could then have the two pleasures. But Denzil was stopped halfway through the door.

"Ticket, sir!"

Denzil drew himself up to his full height.

"Press," he said majestically. All the glories and grandeurs of the Fourth Estate were concentrated in that haughty monosyllable. Heaven itself is full of journalists who have overawed St. Peter. But the doorkeeper was a veritable dragon.

"What paper, sir?"

"*New York Herald*" said Denzil, sharply. He did not relish his word being distrusted.

"*New York Herald*" said one of the bystanding stewards, scarce catching the sounds. "Pass him in."

And in the twinkling of an eye Denzil had eagerly slipped inside.

But during the brief altercation Wimp had come up. Even he could not make his face quite impassive, and there was a suppressed intensity in the eyes and a quiver about the mouth. He went in on Denzil's heels, blocking up the doorway with Grodman. The two men were so full of their coming *coups* that they struggled for some seconds, side by side, before they recognized each other. Then they shook hands heartily.

"That was Cantercot just went in, wasn't it, Grodman?" said Wimp.

"I didn't notice," said Grodman, in tones of utter indifference.

At bottom Wimp was terribly excited. He felt that his *coup* was going to be executed under very sensational circumstances. Everything would combine to turn the eyes of the country upon him - nay, of the world, for had not the Big Bow Mystery been discussed in every language under the sun? In these electric times the criminal receives a cosmopolitan reputation. It is a privilege he shares with few other artists. This time Wimp would be one of them. And he felt deservedly so. If the criminal had been cunning to the point of genius in planning the murder, he had been acute to the point of divination in detecting it. Never before had he pieced together so broken a chain. He could not resist the unique opportunity of setting a sensational scheme in a sensational framework. The dramatic instinct was strong in him; he felt like a playwright who has constructed a strong melodramatic plot, and has the Drury Lane stage suddenly offered him to present it on. It would be folly to deny himself the luxury, though the presence of Mr. Gladstone and the nature of the ceremony should perhaps have given him pause. Yet, on the other hand, these were the very factors of the temptation. Wimp went in and took a seat behind Denzil. All the seats were numbered, so that everybody might have the satisfaction of occupying somebody else's. Denzil was in the special reserved places in the front row just by the central gangway; Crowl was squeezed into a corner behind a pillar near the back of the hall.

Grodman had been honored with a seat on the platform, which was accessible by steps on the right and left, but he kept his eye on Denzil. The picture of the poor idealist hung on the wall behind Grodman's head, covered by its curtain of brown holland. There was a subdued buzz of excitement about the hall, which swelled into cheers every now and again as some gentleman known to fame or Bow took his place upon the platform. It was occupied by several local M.P.'s of varying politics, a number of other Parliamentary satellites of the great man, three or four labor leaders, a peer or two of philanthropic pretensions, a sprinkling of Toynbee and Oxford Hall men, the president and other honorary officials, some of the family and friends of the deceased, together with the inevitable percentage of persons who had no claim to be there save cheek.

Gladstone was late - later than Mortlake, who was cheered to the echo when he arrived, someone starting "For He's a Jolly Good Fellow," as if it were a political meeting. Gladstone came in just in time to acknowledge the compliment. The noise of the song, trolled out from iron lungs, had drowned the huzzahs heralding the old man's advent. The convivial chorus went to Mortlake's head, as if champagne had really preceded it. His eyes grew moist and dim. He saw himself swimming to the Millennium on waves of enthusiasm. Ah, how his brother toilers should be rewarded for their trust in him!

With his usual courtesy and consideration, Mr. Gladstone had refused to perform the actual unveiling of Arthur Constant's portrait. "That," he said in his postcard, "will fall most appropriately to Mr. Mortlake, a gentleman who has, I am given to understand, enjoyed the personal friendship of the late Mr. Constant, and has cooperated with him in various schemes for the organization of skilled and unskilled classes of labor, as well as for the diffusion of better ideals - ideals of self-culture and self-restraint - among the working men of Bow, who have been fortunate, so far as I can perceive, in the possession (if in one case unhappily only temporary possession) of two such men of undoubted ability and honesty to direct their divided counsels and to lead them along a road, which, though I cannot pledge myself to approve of it in all its turnings and windings, is yet not unfitted to bring them somewhat nearer to goals to which there are few of us but would extend some measure of hope that the working classes of this great Empire may in due course, yet with no unnecessary delay, be enabled to arrive."

Mr. Gladstone's speech was an expansion of his postcard, punctuated by cheers. The only new thing in it was the graceful and touching way in which he revealed what had been a secret up till then - that the portrait had been painted and presented to the Bow Break o' Day Club by Lucy Brent, who in the fullness of time would have been Arthur Constant's wife. It was a painting for which he had sat to her while alive, and she had stifled yet pampered her grief by working hard at it since his death. The fact added the last touch of pathos to the occasion. Crowl's face was hidden behind his red handkerchief; even the fire of excitement in Wimp's eye was quenched for a moment by a teardrop, as he thought of Mrs. Wimp and Wilfred. As for Grodman, there was almost a lump in his throat. Denzil Cantercot was the only unmoved man in the room. He thought the episode quite too Beautiful, and was already weaving it into rhyme.

At the conclusion of his speech Mr. Gladstone called upon Tom Mortlake to unveil the portrait. Tom rose, pale and excited. He faltered as he touched the cord. He seemed overcome with emotion. Was it the mention of Lucy Brent that had moved him to his depths?

The brown holland fell away; the dead stood revealed as he had been in life. Every feature, painted by the hand of Love, was instinct with vitality: the fine, earnest face, the sad kindly eyes, the noble brow, seeming still a-throb with the thought of Humanity. A thrill ran through the room; there was a low, undefinable murmur. Oh, the pathos and the tragedy of it! Every eye was fixed, misty with emotion, upon the dead man in the picture, and the living man who stood, pale and agitated, and visibly unable to commence his speech, at the side of the canvas. Suddenly a hand was laid upon the labor leader's shoulder, and there rang through the hall in Wimp's clear, decisive tones the words: "Tom Mortlake, I arrest you for the murder of Arthur Constant!"

IX

For a moment there was an acute, terrible silence. Mortlake's face was that of a corpse; the face of the dead man at his side was flushed with the hues of life. To the overstrung nerves of the onlookers, the brooding eyes of the picture seemed sad and stern with menace, and charged with the lightnings of doom.

It was a horrible contrast. For Wimp, alone, the painted face had fuller, more tragical meanings. The audience seemed turned to stone. They sat or stood in every variety of attitude; frozen, rigid. Arthur Constant's picture dominated the scene, the only living thing in a hall of the dead.

But only for a moment. Mortlake shook off the detective's hand.

"Boys!" he cried, in accents of infinite indignation, "this is a police conspiracy."

His words relaxed the tension. The stony figures were agitated. A dull excited hubbub answered him. The little cobbler darted from behind his pillar, and leapt upon a bench. The cords of his brow were swollen with excitement. He seemed a giant overshadowing the hall.

"Boys!" he roared, in his best Victoria Park voice, "listen to me. This charge is a foul and damnable lie."

"Bravo!"

"Hear! Hear!"

"Hooray!"

"It is!" was roared back at him from all parts of the room. Everybody rose and stood in tentative attitudes, excited to the last degree.

"Boys!" Peter roared on, "you all know me. I'm a plain man, and I want to know if it's likely a man would murder his best friend."

"No!" in a mighty volume of sound.

Wimp had scarcely calculated upon Mortlake's popularity. He stood on the platform, pale and anxious as his prisoner.

"And if he did, why didn't they prove it the first time?"

"Hear, Hear!"

"And if they want to arrest him, why couldn't they leave it till the ceremony was over? Tom Mortlake's not the man to run away."

"Tom Mortlake! Tom Mortlake! Three cheers for Tom Mortlake!"

"Hip, hip, hip, hooray!"

"Three groans for the police!"

"Hoo! Oo! Oo!"

Wimp's melodrama was not going well. He felt like the author to whose ears is borne the ominous sibilance of the pit. He almost wished he had not followed the curtain raiser with his own stronger drama. Unconsciously the police, scattered about the hall, drew together. The people on the platform knew not what to do. They had all risen and stood in a densely packed mass. Even Mr. Gladstone's speech failed him in circumstances so novel. The groans died away; the cheers for Mortlake rose and swelled and fell and rose again. Sticks and umbrellas were banged and rattled, handkerchiefs were waved, the thunder deepened. The motley crowd, still surging about the hall took up the cheers, and for hundreds of yards around people were going black in the face out of mere irresponsible enthusiasm. At last Tom waved his hand; the thunder dwindled, died.

The prisoner was master of the situation.

Grodman stood on the platform, grasping the back of his chair, a curious mocking Mephistophelian glitter about his eyes, his lips wreathed into a half smile. There was no hurry for him to get Denzil Cantercot arrested now. Wimp had made an egregious, a colossal blunder. In Grodman's heart there was a great, glad calm as of a man who has strained his sinews to win in a famous match, and has heard the judge's word. He felt almost kindly to Denzil now.

Tom Mortlake spoke. His face was set and stony. His tall figure was drawn up haughtily to its full height. He pushed the black mane back from his forehead with a characteristic gesture. The fevered audience hung upon his lips. The men at the back leaned eagerly forward. The reporters were breathless with fear lest they should miss a word. What would the great labor leader have to say at this supreme moment?

"Mr. Chairman and gentlemen. It is to me a melancholy pleasure to have been honored with the task of unveiling tonight this portrait of a great benefactor to Bow and a true friend to the laboring classes. Except that he honored me with his friendship while living, and that the aspirations of my life have, in my small and restricted way, been identical with his, there is little reason why this honorable duty should have fallen upon me. Gentlemen, I trust that we shall all find an inspiring influence in the daily vision of the dead, who yet liveth in our hearts and in this noble work of art; wrought, as Mr. Gladstone has told us, by the hand of one who loved him." The speaker paused a moment, his low vibrant tones faltering into silence. "If we humble working men of Bow can never hope to exert individually a tithe of the beneficial influence wielded by Arthur Constant, it is yet possible for each of us to walk in the light he has kindled in our midst - a perpetual lamp of self-sacrifice and brotherhood."

That was all. The room rang with cheers. Tom Mortlake resumed his seat. To Wimp the man's audacity verged on the Sublime; to Denzil on the Beautiful. Again there was a breathless hush. Mr. Gladstone's mobile face was working with excitement. No such extraordinary scene had occurred in the whole of his extraordinary experience. He seemed about to rise. The cheering subsided to a painful stillness. Wimp cut the situation by laying his hand again upon Tom's shoulder.

"Come quietly with me," he said. The words were almost a whisper, but in the supreme silence they traveled to the ends of the hall.

"Don't you go, Tom!" The trumpet tones were Peter's. The call thrilled an answering chord of defiance in every breast, and a low ominous murmur swept through the hall.

Tom rose, and there was silence again. "Boys," he said, "let me go. Don't make any noise about it. I shall be with you again tomorrow."

But the blood of the Break o' Day boys was at fever heat. A hurtling mass of men struggled confusedly from their seats. In a moment all was chaos. Tom did not move. Half-a-dozen men headed by Peter scaled the platform. Wimp was thrown to one side, and the invaders formed a ring round Tom's chair. The platform people scampered like mice from the center. Some huddled together in the corners, others slipped out at the rear. The committee congratulated themselves on having had the self-denial to exclude ladies. Mr. Gladstone's satellites hurried the old man off and into his carriage, though the fight promised to become Homeric. Grodman stood at the side of the platform secretly more amused than ever, concerning himself no more with Denzil Cantercot, who was already strengthening his nerves at the bar upstairs. The police about the hall blew their whistles, and policemen came rushing in from outside and the neighborhood. An Irish M.P. on the platform was waving his gingham like a shillelagh in sheer excitement, forgetting his new-found respectability and dreaming himself back at Donnybrook Fair. Him a conscientious constable floored with a truncheon. But a shower of fists fell on the zealot's face, and he tottered back bleeding.

Then the storm broke in all its fury. The upper air was black with staves, sticks, and umbrellas, mingled with the pallid hailstones of knobby fists. Yells and groans and hoots and battle cries blent in grotesque chorus - like one of Dvorak's weird diabolical movements. Mortlake stood impassive, with arms folded, making no further effort, and the battle raged round him as the water swirls round some steadfast rock. A posse of police from the back fought their way steadily towards him, and charged up the heights of the platform steps, only to be sent tumbling backwards, as their leader was hurled at them like a battering ram. Upon the top of the heap he fell, surmounting the strata of policemen. But others clambered upon them, escalading the platform. A moment more and Mortlake would have been taken. Then the miracle happened.

As when of old a reputable goddess *ex machina* saw her favorite hero in dire peril, straightway she drew down a cloud from the celestial stores of Jupiter and enveloped her fondling in kindly night, so that his adversary strove with the darkness, so did Crowl, the cunning cobbler, the much-daring, essay to ensure his friend's safety. He turned off the gas at the meter.

An Arctic night - unpreceded by twilight - fell and there dawned the sabbath of the witches. The darkness could be felt - and it left blood and bruises behind it. When the lights were turned on again, Mortlake was gone. But several of the rioters were arrested, triumphantly.

And through all, and over all, the face of the dead man, who had sought to bring peace on earth, brooded.

Crowl sat meekly eating his supper of bread and cheese, with his head bandaged, while Denzil Cantercot told him the story of how he had rescued Tom Mortlake. He had been among the first to scale the height, and had never budged from Tom's side or from the forefront of the battle till he had seen him safely outside and into a by-street.

"I am so glad you saw that he got away safely," said Crowl, "I wasn't quite sure he would."

"Yes; but I wish some cowardly fool hadn't turned off the gas. I like men to *see* that they are beaten."

"But it seemed...easier," faltered Crowl.

"Easier!" echoed Denzil, taking a deep draught of bitter. "Really, Peter, I'm sorry to find you always will take such low views. It may be easier, but it's shabby. It shocks one's sense of the Beautiful."

Crowl ate his bread and cheese shamefacedly.

"But what was the use of breaking your head to save him?" said Mrs. Crowl, with an unconscious pun. "He must be caught."

"Ah, I don't see how the Useful *does* come in, now," said Peter thoughtfully. "But I didn't think of that at the time."

He swallowed his water quickly, and it went the wrong way and added to his confusion. It also began to dawn upon him that he might be called to account. Let it be said at once that he wasn't. He had taken too prominent a part.

Meantime, Mrs. Wimp was bathing Mr. Wimp's eye, and rubbing him generally with arnica. Wimp's melodrama had been, indeed, a sight for the gods. Only virtue was vanquished and vice triumphant. The villain had escaped, and without striking a blow.

X

There was matter and to spare for the papers the next day. The striking ceremony - Mr. Gladstone's speech - the sensational arrest - these would of themselves have made excellent themes for reports and leaders. But the personality of the man arrested, and the Big Bow Mystery Battle - as it came to be called - gave additional piquancy to the paragraphs and the posters. The behavior of Mortlake put the last touch to the picturesqueness of the position. He left the hall when the lights went out, and walked unnoticed and unmolested through pleiads of policemen to the nearest police station, where the superintendent was almost too excited to take any notice of his demand to be arrested. But to do him justice, the official yielded as soon as he understood the situation. It seems inconceivable that he did not violate some red-tape regulation in so doing. To some this self surrender was limpid proof of innocence; to others it was the damning token of despairing guilt.

The morning papers were pleasant reading for Grodman, who chuckled as continuously over his morning egg, as if he had laid it. Jane was alarmed for the sanity of her saturnine master. As her husband would have said, Grodman's grins were not Beautiful. But he made no effort to suppress them. Not only had Wimp perpetrated a grotesque blunder, but the journalists to a man were down on his great sensation tableau, though their denunciations did not appear in the dramatic columns. The Liberal papers said that he had endangered Mr. Gladstone's life; the Conservative that he had unloosed the raging elements of Bow blackguardism, and set in motion forces which might have easily swelled to a riot, involving severe destruction of property. But "Tom Mortlake" was, after all, the thought swamping every other. It was, in a sense, a triumph for the man.

But Wimp's turn came when Mortlake, who reserved his defense, was brought up before a magistrate, and by force of the new evidence, fully committed for trial on the charge of murdering Arthur Constant. Then men's thoughts centered again on the Mystery, and the solution of the inexplicable problem agitated mankind from China to Peru.

In the middle of February, the great trial befell. It was another of the opportunities which the Chancellor of the Excheckr neglects. So stirring a drama might have easily cleared its expenses - despite the length of the cast, the salaries of the stars, and the rent of the house - in mere advance booking. For it was a drama which (by the rights of Magna Charta) could never be repeated; a drama which ladies of fashion would have given their earrings to witness, even with the central figure not a woman. And there *was* a woman in it anyhow, to judge by the little that had transpired at the magisterial examination, and the fact that the country was placarded with bills offering a reward for information concerning a Miss Jessie Dymond. Mortlake was defended by Sir Charles Brown-Harland, Q.C., retained at the expense of the Mortlake Defense Fund (subscriptions to which came also from Australia and the Continent) and set on his mettle by the fact that he was the accepted labor candidate for an East-end constituency. Their Majesties, Victoria and the Law, were represented by Mr. Robert Spigot, Q.C.

Mr. SPIGOT, Q.C, in presenting his case, said: "I propose to show that the prisoner murdered his friend and fellow-lodger, Mr. Arthur Constant, in cold blood, and with the most careful premeditation; premeditation so studied, as to leave the circumstances of the death an impenetrable mystery for weeks to all the world though, fortunately, without altogether baffling the almost superhuman ingenuity of Mr. Edward Wimp of the Scotland Yard Detective Department. I propose to show that the motives of the prisoner were jealousy and revenge; jealousy not only of his friend's superior influence over the working men he himself aspired to lead, but the more commonplace animosity engendered by the disturbing element of a woman having relations to both. If, before my case is complete, it will be my painful duty to show that the murdered man was not the saint the world has agreed to paint him, I shall not shrink from unveiling the truer picture, in the interests of justice, which cannot say *nil nisi bonum* even of the dead. I propose to show that the murder was committed by the prisoner shortly before half-past six on the morning of December 4th, and that the prisoner having, with the remarkable ingenuity which he has shown throughout, attempted to prepare an alibi by feigning to leave London by the *first* train to Liverpool, returned home, got in with his latchkey through the street door, which he had left on the latch, unlocked his victim's bedroom with a key which he possessed, cut the sleeping man's throat, pocketed his razor, locked the door again, and gave it the appearance of being bolted, went downstairs, unslipped the bolt of the big lock, closed the door behind him and got to Euston in time for the *second* train to Liverpool. The fog helped his proceedings throughout." Such was in sum the theory of the prosecution. The pale, defiant figure in the dock winced perceptibly under parts of it.

Mrs. Drabdump was the first witness called for the prosecution. She was quite used to legal inquisitiveness by this time, but did not appear in good spirits.

"On the night of December 3rd, you gave the prisoner a letter?"

"Yes, your ludship."

"How did he behave when he read it?"

"He turned very pale and excited. He went up to the poor gentleman's room, and I'm afraid he quarreled with him. He might have left his last hours peaceful." (Amusement.)

"What happened then?"

"Mr. Mortlake went out in a passion, and came in again in about an hour."

"He told you he was going away to Liverpool very early the next morning?"

"No, your ludship, he said he was going to Devonport." (Sensation.)

"What time did you get up the next morning?"

"Half-past six."

"That is not your usual time?"

"No, I always get up at six."

"How do you account for the extra sleepiness?"

"Misfortunes will happen."

"It wasn't the dull, foggy weather?"

"No, my lud, else I should never get up early." (Laughter.)

"You drink something before going to bed?"

"I like my cup o' tea. I take it strong, without sugar. It always steadies my nerves."

"Quite so. Where were you when the prisoner told you he was going to Devonport?"

"Drinkin' my tea in the kitchen."

"What should you say if prisoner dropped something in it to make you sleep late?"

WITNESS (startled): "He ought to be shot."

"He might have done it without your noticing it, I suppose?"

"If he was clever enough to murder the poor gentleman, he was clever enough to try and poison me."

The JUDGE: "The witness in her replies must confine herself to the evidence."

Mr. SPIGOT, Q.C.: "I must submit to your lordship that it is a very logical answer, and exactly illustrates the interdependence of the probabilities. Now, Mrs. Drabdump, let us know what happened when you awoke at half-past six the next morning."

Thereupon Mrs. Drabdump recapitulated the evidence (with new redundancies, but slight variations) given by her at the inquest. How she became alarmed - how she found the street door locked by the big lock - how she roused Grodman and got him to burst open the door - how they found the body - all this with which the public was already familiar *ad nauseam* was extorted from her afresh.

"Look at this key (key passed to witness). Do you recognize it?"

"Yes; how did you get it? It's the key of my first floor front. I am sure I left it sticking in the door."

"Did you know a Miss Dymond?"

"Yes, Mr. Mortlake's sweetheart. But I knew he would never marry her, poor thing." (Sensation.)

"Why not?"

"He was getting too grand for her." (Amusement.)

"You don't mean anything more than that?"

131

"I don't know; she only came to my place once or twice. The last time I set eyes on her must have been in October."

"How did she appear?"

"She was very miserable, but she wouldn't let you see it." (Laughter.)

"How has the prisoner behaved since the murder?"

"He always seemed very glum and sorry for it."

Cross-Examined: "Did not the prisoner once occupy the bedroom of Mr. Constant, and give it up to him, so that Mr. Constant might have the two rooms on the same floor?"

"Yes, but he didn't pay as much."

"And, while occupying this front bedroom, did not the prisoner once lose his key and have another made?"

"He did; he was very careless."

"Do you know what the prisoner and Mr. Constant spoke about on the night of December 3rd?"

"No; I couldn't hear."

"Then how did you know they were quarrelling?"

"They were talkin' so loud."

Sir CHARLES BROWN-HARLAND, Q.C. (sharply): "But I'm talking loudly to you now. Should you say I was quarrelling?"

"It takes two to make a quarrel." (Laughter.)

"Was prisoner the sort of man who, in your opinion, would commit a murder?"

"No, I never should ha' guessed it was him."

"He always struck you as a thorough gentleman?"

"No, my lud. I knew he was only a comp."

"You say the prisoner has seemed depressed since the murder. Might not that have been due to the disappearance of his sweetheart?"

"No, he'd more likely be glad to get rid of her."

"Then he wouldn't be jealous if Mr. Constant took her off his hands?" (Sensation.)

"Men are dog-in-the-mangers."

"Never mind about men, Mrs. Drabdump. Had the prisoner ceased to care for Miss Dymond?"

"He didn't seem to think of her, my lud. When he got a letter in her handwriting among his heap he used to throw it aside till he'd torn open the others."

BROWN-HARLAND, Q.C. (with a triumphant ring in his voice): "Thank you, Mrs. Drabdump. You may sit down."

SPIGOT, Q.C.: "One moment, Mrs. Drabdump. You say the prisoner had ceased to care for Miss Dymond. Might not this have been in consequence of his suspecting for some time that she had relations with Mr. Constant?"

The JUDGE: "That is not a fair question."

SPIGOT, Q.C.: "That will do, thank you, Mrs. Drabdump."

BROWN-HARLAND, Q.C.: "No; one question more, Mrs. Drabdump. Did you ever see anything - say, when Miss Dymond came to your house - to make you suspect anything between Mr. Constant and the prisoner's sweetheart?"

"She did meet him once when Mr. Mortlake was out." (Sensation.)

"Where did she meet him?"

"In the passage. He was going out when she knocked and he opened the door." (Amusement.)

"You didn't hear what they said?"

"I ain't a eavesdropper. They spoke friendly and went away together."

Mr. GEORGE GRODMAN was called, and repeated his evidence at the inquest. Cross-examined, he testified to the warm friendship between Mr. Constant and the prisoner. He knew very little about Miss Dymond, having scarcely seen her. Prisoner had never spoken to him much about her. He should not think she was much in prisoner's thoughts. Naturally the prisoner had been depressed by the death of his friend. Besides, he was overworked. Witness thought highly of Mortlake's character. It was incredible that Constant had had improper relations of any kind with his friend's promised wife. Grodman's evidence made a very favorable impression on the jury; the prisoner looked his gratitude; and the prosecution felt sorry it had been necessary to call this witness.

Inspector HOWLETT and Sergeant RUNNYMEDE had also to repeat their evidence. Dr. ROBINSON, police surgeon, likewise retendered his evidence as to the nature of the wound, and the approximate hour of death. But this time he was much more severely examined. He would not bind himself down to state the time within an hour or two. He thought life had been extinct two or three hours when he arrived, so that the deed had been committed between seven and eight. Under gentle pressure from the prosecuting counsel, he admitted that it might possibly have been between six and seven. Cross-examined, he reiterated his impression in favor of the later hour.

Supplementary evidence from medical experts proved as dubious and uncertain as if the court had confined itself to the original witness. It seemed to be generally agreed that the data for determining the time of death of any body were too complex and variable to admit of very precise inference; rigor mortis and other symptoms setting in within very wide limits and differing largely in different persons. All agreed that death from such a cut must have been practically instantaneous, and the theory of suicide was rejected by all. As a whole the medical evidence tended to fix the time of death, with a high degree of probability, between the hours of six and half-past eight. The efforts of the prosecution were bent upon throwing back the time of death to as early as possible after about half-past five. The defense spent all its strength upon pinning the experts to the conclusion that death could not have been earlier than seven. Evidently the prosecution was going to fight hard for the hypothesis that Mortlake had committed the crime in the interval between the first and second trains for Liverpool; while the defense was concentrating itself on an alibi, showing that the prisoner had traveled by the second train which left Euston Station at a quarter-past seven, so that there could have been no possible time for the passage between Bow and Euston. It was an exciting struggle. As yet the contending forces seemed equally matched. The evidence had gone as much for as against the prisoner. But everybody knew that worse lay behind.

"Call Edward Wimp."

The story EDWARD WIMP had to tell began tamely enough with thrice-threshed-out facts. But at last the new facts came.

"In consequence of suspicions that had formed in your mind you took up your quarters, disguised, in the late Mr. Constant's rooms?"

"I did; at the commencement of the year. My suspicions had gradually gathered against the occupants of No. 11 Glover Street, and I resolved to quash or confirm these suspicions once for all."

"Will you tell the jury what followed?"

"Whenever the prisoner was away for the night I searched his room. I found the key of Mr. Constant's bedroom buried deeply in the side of prisoner's leather sofa. I found what I imagine to be the letter he received on December 3rd, in the pages of a 'Bradshaw' lying under the same sofa. There were two razors about."

Mr. SPIGOT, Q.C., said: "The key has already been identified by Mrs. Drabdump. The letter I now propose to read."

It was undated, and ran as follows:

Dear Tom,

This is to bid you farewell. It is best for us all. I am going a long way dearest. Do not seek to find me, for it will be useless. Think of me as one swallowed up by the waters, and be assured that it is only to spare you shame and humiliation in the future that I tear myself from you and all the sweetness of life. Darling, there is no other way. I feel you could never marry me now. I have felt it for months. Dear Tom, you will understand what I mean. We must look facts in the face. I hope you will always be friends with Mr. Constant. Goodbye, dear. God bless you!

May you always be happy, and find a worthier wife than I. Perhaps when you are great and rich and famous as you deserve, you will sometimes think not unkindly of one who, however faulty and unworthy of you, will at least love you till the end.

Yours, till death,

JESSIE.

By the time this letter was finished numerous old gentlemen, with wigs or without, were observed to be polishing their glasses. Mr. Wimp's examination was resumed.

"After making these discoveries what did you do?"

"I made inquiries about Miss Dymond, and found Mr. Constant had visited her once or twice in the evening. I imagined there would be some traces of a pecuniary connection. I was allowed by the family to inspect Mr. Constant's checkbook, and found a paid check made out for L25 in the name of Miss Dymond. By inquiry at the Bank, I found it had been cashed on

November 12th of last year. I then applied for a warrant against the prisoner."

Cross-examined: "Do you suggest that the prisoner opened Mr. Constant's bedroom with the key you found?"

"Certainly."

BROWN-HARLAND, Q.C. (sarcastically): "And locked the door from within with it on leaving?"

"Certainly."

"Will you have the goodness to explain how the trick was done?"

"It wasn't done. (Laughter.) The prisoner probably locked the door from the outside. Those who broke it open naturally imagined it had been locked from the inside when they found the key inside. The key would, on this theory, be on the floor as the outside locking could not have been effected if it had been in the lock. The first persons to enter the room would naturally believe it had been thrown down in the bursting of the door. Or it might have been left sticking very loosely inside the lock so as not to interfere with the turning of the outside key, in which case it would also probably have been thrown to the ground."

"Indeed. Very ingenious. And can you also explain how the prisoner could have bolted the door within from the outside?"

"I can. (Renewed sensation.) There is only one way in which it was possible and that was, of course, a mere conjurer's illusion. To cause a locked door to appear bolted in addition, it would only be necessary for the person on the inside of the door to wrest the staple containing the bolt from the woodwork. The bolt in Mr. Constant's bedroom worked perpendicularly. When the staple was torn off, it would simply remain at rest on the pin of the bolt instead of supporting it or keeping it fixed. A person bursting open the door and finding the staple resting on the pin and torn away from the lintel of the door would, of course, imagine he had torn it away, never dreaming the wresting off had been done beforehand." (Applause in court, which was instantly checked by the ushers.) The counsel for the defense felt he had been entrapped in attempting to be sarcastic with the redoubtable detective. Grodman seemed green with envy. It was the one thing he had not thought of.

Mrs. Drabdump, Grodman, Inspector Howlett, and Sergeant Runnymede were recalled and reexammed by the embarrassed Sir Charles Brown-Harland as to the exact condition of the lock and the bolt and the position of the key. It turned out as Wimp had suggested; so prepossessed were the witnesses with the conviction that the door was locked and bolted from the inside when it was burst open that they were a little hazy about the exact details. The damage had been repaired, so that it was all a question of precise past observation. The inspector and the sergeant testified that the key was in the lock when they saw it, though both the mortise and the bolt were broken. They were not prepared to say that Wimp's theory was impossible; they would even admit it was quite possible that the staple of the bolt had been torn off beforehand. Mrs. Drabdump could give no clear account of such petty facts in view of her immediate engrossing interest in the horrible sight of the corpse. Grodman alone was positive that the key was in the door when he burst it open. No, he did not remember picking it up from the floor and putting it in. And he was certain that the staple of the bolt was *not* broken, from the resistance he experienced in trying to shake the upper panels of the door.

By the Prosecution: "Don't you think, from the comparative ease with which the door yielded to your onslaught, that it is highly probable that the pin of the bolt was not in a firmly fixed staple, but in one already detached from the woodwork of the lintel?"

"The door did not yield so easily."

"But you must be a Hercules."

"Not quite; the bolt was old, and the woodwork crumbling; the lock was new and shoddy. But I have always been a strong man."

"Very well, Mr. Grodman. I hope you will never appear at the music halls." (Laughter.)

Jessie Dymond's landlady was the next witness for the prosecution. She corroborated Wimp's statements as to Constant's occasional visits, and narrated how the girl had been enlisted by the dead philanthropist as a collaborator in some of his enterprises. But the most telling portion of her evidence was the story of how, late at night, on December 3rd, the prisoner called upon her and inquired wildly about the whereabouts of his sweetheart. He said he had just received a mysterious letter from Miss Dymond saying she was gone. She (the landlady) replied that she could have told him that weeks ago, as her ungrateful lodger was gone now some three weeks without leaving a hint behind her. In answer to his most ungentlemanly raging and raving, she told him it served him right, as he should have looked after her better, and not kept away for so long. She reminded him that there were as good fish in the sea as ever came out, and a girl of Jessie's attractions need not pine away (as she had seemed to be pining away) for lack of appreciation. He then called her a liar and left her, and she hoped never to see his face again, though she was not surprised to see it in the dock.

Mr. FITZJAMES MONTGOMERY, a bank clerk, remembered cashing the check produced. He particularly remembered it, because he paid the money to a very pretty girl. She took the entire amount in gold. At this point the case was adjourned.

DENZIL CANTERCOT was the first witness called for the prosecution on the resumption of the trial. Pressed as to whether he had not told Mr. Wimp that he had overheard the prisoner denouncing Mr. Constant, he could not say. He had not actually heard the prisoner's denunciations; he might have given Mr. Wimp a false impression, but then Mr. Wimp was so prosaically literal. (Laughter.) Mr. Crowl had told him something of the kind. Cross-examined, he said Jessie Dymond was a rare spirit and she always reminded him of Joan of Arc.

Mr. CROWL, being called, was extremely agitated. He refused to take the oath, and informed the court that the Bible was a Fad. He could not swear by anything so self-contradictory. He would affirm. He could not deny - though he looked like wishing to - that the prisoner had at first been rather mistrustful of Mr. Constant, but he was certain that the feeling had quickly worn off. Yes, he was a great friend of the prisoner, but he didn't see why that should invalidate his testimony, especially as he had not taken an oath. Certainly the prisoner seemed rather depressed when he saw him on Bank Holiday, but it was overwork on behalf of the people and for the demolition of the Fads.

Several other familiars of the prisoner gave more or less reluctant testimony as to his sometime prejudice against the amateur rival labor leader. His expressions of dislike had been strong and bitter. The prosecution also produced a poster announcing that the prisoner would preside at a great meeting of clerks on December 4th. He had not turned up at this meeting nor sent any explanation. Finally, there was the evidence of the detectives who originally arrested him at Liverpool Docks in view of his suspicious demeanor. This completed the case for the prosecution.

Sir CHARLES BROWN-HARLAND, Q.C., rose with a swagger and a rustle of his silk gown, and proceeded to set forth the theory of the defense. He said he did not purpose to call many witnesses. The hypothesis of the prosecution was so inherently childish and inconsequential, and so dependent upon a bundle of interdependent probabilities that it crumbled away at the merest touch. The prisoner's character was of unblemished integrity, his last public appearance had been made on the same platform with Mr. Gladstone, and his honesty and high mindedness had been vouched for by statesmen of the highest standing. His movements could be accounted for from hour to hour - and those with which the prosecution credited him rested on no tangible evidence whatever. He was also credited with superhuman ingenuity and diabolical cunning of which he had shown no previous symptom. Hypothesis was piled on hypothesis, as in the old Oriental legend, where the world rested on the elephant and the elephant on the tortoise. It might be worth while, however, to point out that it was at least quite likely that the death of Mr. Constant had not taken place before seven, and as the prisoner left Euston Station at 7:15 a.m. for Liverpool, he could certainly not have got there from Bow in the time; also that it was hardly possible for the prisoner, who could prove being at Euston Station at 5.25 a.m., to travel backwards and forwards to Glover Street and commit the crime all within less than two hours.

"The real facts," said Sir Charles, impressively, "are most simple. The prisoner, partly from pressure of work, partly (he had no wish to conceal) from worldly ambition, had begun to neglect Miss Dymond, to whom he was engaged to be married. The man was but human, and his head was a little turned by his growing importance. Nevertheless, at heart he was still deeply attached to Miss Dymond. She, however, appears to have jumped to the conclusion that he had ceased to love her, that she was unworthy of him, unfitted by education to take her place side by side with him in the new spheres to which he was mounting - that, in short, she was a drag on his career. Being, by all accounts, a girl of remarkable force of character, she resolved to cut the Gordian knot by leaving London, and, fearing lest her affianced husband's conscientiousness should induce him to sacrifice himself to her; dreading also, perhaps, her own weakness, she made the parting absolute, and the place of her refuge a mystery. A theory has been suggested which drags an honored name in the mire; a theory so superfluous that I shall only allude to it. That Arthur Constant could have seduced or had any improper relations with his friend's betrothed is a hypothesis to which the lives of both give the lie.

Before leaving London - or England - Miss Dymond wrote to her aunt in Devonport - her only living relative in this country - asking her as a great favor to forward an addressed letter to the prisoner, a fortnight after receipt. The aunt obeyed implicitly. This was the letter which fell like a thunderbolt on the prisoner on the night of December 3rd. All his old love returned; he was full of self-reproach and pity for the poor girl. The letter read ominously. Perhaps she was going to put an end to herself. His first thought was to rush up to his friend, Constant, to seek his advice. Perhaps Constant knew something of the affair. The prisoner knew the two were in not infrequent communication. It is possible - my lord and gentlemen of the jury, I do not wish to follow the methods of the prosecution and confuse theory with fact, so I say it is possible - that Mr. Constant had supplied her with the 25 pounds to leave the country. He was like a brother to her, perhaps even acted imprudently in calling upon her, though neither dreamed of evil. It is possible that he may have encouraged her in her abnegation and in her altruistic aspirations, perhaps even without knowing their exact drift, for does he not speak in his very last letter of the fine female characters he was meeting, and the influence for good he had over individual human souls? Still, this we can now never know, unless the dead speak or the absent return. It is also not impossible that Miss Dymond was entrusted with the 25 pounds for charitable purposes. But to come back to certainties. The prisoner consulted Mr. Constant about the letter. He then ran to Miss Dymond's lodgings in Stepney Green, knowing beforehand his trouble would be futile. The letter bore the postmark of Devonport. He knew the girl had an aunt there; possibly she might have gone to her. He could not telegraph, for he was ignorant of the address. He consulted his 'Bradshaw,' and resolved to leave by the 5.30 a.m. from Paddington and told his landlady so.

He left the letter in the 'Bradshaw,' which ultimately got thrust among a pile of papers under the sofa, so that he had to get another. He was careless and disorderly, and the key found by Mr. Wimp in his sofa, which he was absurdly supposed to have hidden there after the murder, must have lain there for some years, having been lost there in the days when he occupied the bedroom afterwards rented by Mr. Constant. For it was his own sofa, removed from that room, and the suction of sofas was well known. Afraid to miss his train, he did not undress on that distressful night. Meantime the thought occurred to him that Jessie was too clever a girl to leave so easy a trail, and he jumped to the conclusion that she would be going to her married brother in America, and had gone to Devonport merely to bid her aunt farewell. He determined therefore to get to Liverpool, without wasting time at Devonport, to institute inquiries. Not suspecting the delay in the transit of the letter, he thought he might yet stop her, even at the landing stage or on the tender. Unfortunately his cab went slowly in the fog, he missed the first train, and wandered about brooding disconsolately in the mist till the second. At Liverpool his suspicious, excited demeanor procured his momentary arrest. Since then the thought of the lost girl has haunted and broken him. That is the whole, the plain, and the sufficing story."

The effective witnesses for the defense were, indeed, few. It is so hard to prove a negative. There was Jessie's aunt, who bore out the statement of the counsel for the defense. There were the porters who saw him leave Euston by the 7:15 train for Liverpool, and arrive just too late for the 5:15; there was the cabman (2138), who drove him to Euston just in time, he (witness) thought, to catch the 5:15 a.m. Under cross-examination, the cabman got a little confused; he was asked whether, if he really picked up the prisoner at Bow Railway Station at about 4.30, he ought not to have caught the first train at Euston. He said the fog made him drive rather slowly, but admitted the mist was transparent enough to warrant full speed. He also admitted being a strong trade unionist, SPIGOT, Q.C., artfully extorting the admission as if it were of the utmost significance. Finally, there were numerous witnesses of all sorts and conditions to the prisoner's high character, as well as to Arthur Constant's blameless and moral life.

In his closing speech on the third day of the trial, Sir CHARLES pointed out with great exhaustiveness and cogency the flimsiness of the case for the prosecution, the number of hypotheses it involved, and their mutual interdependence. Mrs. Drabdump was a witness whose evidence must be accepted with extreme caution. The jury must remember that she was unable to dissociate her observations from her inferences, and thought that the prisoner and Mr. Constant were quarrelling merely because they were agitated. He dissected her evidence, and showed that it entirely bore out the story of the defense. He asked the jury to bear in mind that no positive evidence (whether of cabmen or others) had been given of the various and complicated movements attributed to the prisoner on the morning of December 4th, between the hours of 5:25 and 7:15 a.m., and that the most important witness on the theory of the prosecution – he meant, of course, Miss Dymond - had not been produced. Even if she were dead, and her body were found, no countenance would be given to the theory of the prosecution, for the mere conviction that her lover had deserted her would be a sufficient explanation of her suicide. Beyond the ambiguous letter, no tittle of evidence of her dishonor - on which the bulk of the case against the prisoner rested - had been adduced. As for the motive of political jealousy, that had been a mere passing cloud. The two men had become fast friends. As to the circumstances of the alleged crime, the medical evidence was on the whole in favor of the time of death being late; and the prisoner had left London at a quarter-past seven. The drugging theory was absurd, and as for the too clever bolt and lock theories, Mr. Grodman, a trained scientific observer, had pooh-poohed them. He would solemnly exhort the jury to remember that if they condemned the prisoner they would not only send an innocent man to an ignominious death on the flimsiest circumstantial evidence, but they would deprive the working men of this country of one of their truest friends and their ablest leader.

The conclusion of Sir Charles's vigorous speech was greeted with irrepressible applause.

Mr. SPIGOT, Q.C., in closing the case for the prosecution, asked the jury to return a verdict against the prisoner for as malicious and premeditated a crime as ever disgraced the annals of any civilized country. His cleverness and education had only been utilized for the devil's ends, while his reputation had been used as a cloak. Everything pointed strongly to the prisoner's guilt. On receiving Miss Dymond's letter announcing her shame, and (probably) her intention to commit suicide, he had hastened upstairs to denounce Constant. He had then rushed to the girl's lodgings and, finding his worst fears confirmed, planned at once his diabolically ingenious scheme of revenge. He told his landlady he was going to Devonport, so that if he bungled, the police would be put temporarily off his track. His real destination was Liverpool, for he intended to leave the country. Lest, however, his plan should break down here, too, he arranged an ingenious alibi by being driven to Euston for the 5:15 train to Liverpool. The cabman would not know he did not intend to go by it, but meant to return to 11 Glover Street, there to perpetrate this foul crime, interruption to which he had possibly barred by drugging his landlady. His presence at Liverpool (whither he really went by the second train) would corroborate the cabman's story. That night he had not undressed nor gone to bed; he had plotted out his devilish scheme till it was perfect; the fog came as an unexpected ally to cover his movements. Jealousy, outraged affection, the desire for revenge, the lust for political power - these were human. They might pity the criminal; they could not find him innocent of the crime.

Mr. Justice CROGIE, summing up, began dead against the prisoner. Reviewing the evidence, he pointed out that plausible hypotheses neatly dove-tailed did not necessarily weaken one another, the fitting so well together of the whole rather making for the truth of the parts. Besides, the case for the prosecution was as far from being all hypothesis as the case for the defense was from excluding hypotheses. The key, the letter, the reluctance to produce the letter, the heated interview with Constant, the misstatement about the prisoner's destination, the flight to Liverpool, the false tale about searching for a "him," the denunciations of Constant, all these were facts.

On the other hand, there were various lacunae and hypotheses in the case for the defense. Even conceding the somewhat dubious alibi afforded by the prisoner's presence at Euston at 5:25 a.m., there was no attempt to account for his movements between that and 7:15 a.m. It was as possible that he returned to Bow as that he lingered about Euston. There was nothing in the medical evidence to make his guilt impossible. Nor was there anything inherently impossible in Constant's yielding to the sudden temptation of a beautiful girl, nor in a working girl deeming herself deserted, temporarily succumbing to the fascinations of a gentleman and regretting it bitterly afterwards. What had become of the girl was a mystery. Hers might have been one of those nameless corpses which the tide swirls up on slimy river banks. The jury must remember too, that the relation might not have actually passed into dishonor, it might have been just grave enough to smite the girl's conscience and to induce her to behave as she had done.

It was enough that her letter should have excited the jealousy of the prisoner. There was one other point which he would like to impress on the jury, and which the counsel for the prosecution had not sufficiently insisted upon. This was that the prisoner's guiltiness was the only plausible solution that had ever been advanced of the Bow Mystery. The medical evidence agreed that Mr. Constant did not die by his own hand.

Someone must therefore have murdered him. The number of people who could have had any possible reason or opportunity to murder him was extremely small. The prisoner had both reason and opportunity. By what logicians called the method of exclusion, suspicion would attach to him on even slight evidence.

The actual evidence was strong and plausible, and now that Mr. Wimp's ingenious theory had enabled them to understand how the door could have been apparently locked and bolted from within, the last difficulty and the last argument for suicide had been removed. The prisoner's guilt was as clear as circumstantial evidence could make it.

If they let him go free, the Bow Mystery might henceforward be placed among the archives of unavenged assassinations. Having thus well-nigh hung the prisoner, the judge wound up by insisting on the high probability of the story for the defense, though that too was dependent in important details upon the prisoner's mere private statements to his counsel. The jury, being by this time sufficiently muddled by his impartiality, were dismissed, with the exhortation to allow due weight to every fact and probability in determining their righteous verdict.

The minutes ran into hours, but the jury did not return. The shadows of night fell across the reeking, fevered court before they announced their verdict:

"Guilty!"

The judge put on his black cap.

The great reception arranged outside was a fiasco; the evening banquet was indefinitely postponed. Wimp had won; Grodman felt like a whipped cur.

<u>XI</u>

"So you were right," Denzil could not help saying as he greeted Grodman a week afterwards. "I shall *not* live to tell the story of how you discovered the Bow murderer."

"Sit down," growled Grodman; "perhaps you will after all." There was a dangerous gleam in his eyes. Denzil was sorry he had spoken.

"I sent for you," Grodman said, "to tell you that on the night Wimp arrested Mortlake I had made preparations for your arrest."

Denzil gasped, "What for?"

"My dear Denzil, there is a little law in this country invented for the confusion of the poetic. The greatest exponent of the Beautiful is only allowed the same number of wives as the green grocer. I do not blame you for not being satisfied with Jane - she is a good servant but a bad mistress - but it was cruel to Kitty not to inform her that Jane had a prior right in you, and unjust to Jane not to let her know of the contract with Kitty."

"They both know it now well enough, curse 'em," said the poet.

"Yes; your secrets are like your situations; you can't keep 'em long. My poor poet, I pity you - betwixt the devil and the deep sea."

"They're a pair of harpies, each holding over me the Damocles sword of an arrest for bigamy. Neither loves me."

"I should think they would come in very useful to you. You plant one in my house to tell my secrets to Wimp, and you plant one in Wimp's house to tell Wimp's secrets to me, I suppose. Out with some, then."

"Upon my honor, you wrong me. Jane brought *me* here, not I Jane. As for Kitty, I never had such a shock in my life as at finding her installed in Wimp's house."

"She thought it safer to have the law handy for your arrest. Besides, she probably desired to occupy a parallel position to Jane's. She must do something for a living; *you* wouldn't do anything for hers. And so you couldn't go anywhere without meeting a wife! Ha! Ha! Ha! Serve you right, my polygamous poet."

"But why should *you* arrest me?"

"Revenge, Denzil. I have been the best friend you ever had in this cold, prosaic world. You have eaten my bread, drunk my claret, written my book, smoked my cigars, and pocketed my money. And yet, when you have an important piece of information bearing on a mystery about which I am thinking day and night, you calmly go and sell it to Wimp."

"I did - didn't," stammered Denzil.

"Liar! Do you think Kitty has any secrets from me? As soon as I discovered your two marriages I determined to have you arrested for your treachery. But when I found you had, as I thought, put Wimp on the wrong scent, when I felt sure that by arresting Mortlake he was going to make a greater ass of himself than even nature had been able to do, then I forgave you. I let you walk about the earth and drink freely. Now it is Wimp who crows; everybody pats him on the back. They call him the mystery man of the Scotland Yard tribe. Poor Tom Mortlake will be hanged, and all through your telling Wimp about Jessie Dymond!"

"It was you yourself," said Denzil, sullenly. "Everybody was giving it up. But you said 'Let us find out all that Arthur Constant did in the last few months of his life.' Wimp couldn't miss stumbling on Jessie sooner or later. I'd have throttled Constant, if I had known he'd touched her," he wound up with irrelevant indignation.

Grodman winced at the idea that he himself had worked *ad majorem gloriam* of Wimp. And yet, had not Mrs. Wimp let out as much at the Christmas dinner?

"What's past is past," he said gruffly. "But if Tom Mortlake hangs, you go to Portland."

"How can I help Tom hanging?"

"Help the agitation as much as you can. Write letters under all sorts of names to all the papers. Get everybody you know to sign the great petition. Find out where Jessie Dymond is; the girl who holds the proof of Mortlake's innocence."

"You really believe him innocent?"

"Don't be satirical, Denzil. Haven't I taken the chair at all the meetings? Am I not the most copious correspondent of the Press?"

"I thought it was only to spite Wimp."

"Rubbish. It's to save poor Tom. He no more murdered Arthur Constant than - you did!" He laughed an unpleasant laugh.

Denzil bade him farewell, frigid with fear.

Grodman was up to his ears in letters and telegrams. Somehow he had become the leader of the rescue party - suggestions, subscriptions came from all sides. The suggestions were burnt, the subscriptions acknowledged in the papers and used for hunting up the missing girl. Lucy Brent headed the list with a hundred pounds. It was a fine testimony to her faith in her dead lover's honor.

The release of the Jury had unloosed "The Greater Jury," which always now sits upon the smaller. Every means was taken to nullify the value of the "palladium of British liberty." The foreman and the jurors were interviewed, the judge was judged and by those who were no judges. The Home Secretary (who had done nothing beyond accepting office under the Crown) was vituperated, and sundry provincial persons wrote confidentially to the Queen. Arthur Constant's backsliding cheered many by convincing them that others were as bad as themselves; and well-to-do tradesmen saw in Mortlake's wickedness the pernicious effects of Socialism. A dozen new theories were afloat. Constant had committed suicide by Esoteric Buddhism, as witness his devotion to Mme. Blavatsky, or he had been murdered by his Mahatma or victimized by Hypnotism, Mesmerism, Somnambulism and other weird abstractions. Grodman's great point was - Jessie Dymond must be produced, dead or alive. The electric current scoured the civilized world in search of her. What wonder if the shrewder sort divined that the indomitable detective had fixed his last hope on the girl's guilt? If Jessie had wrongs why should she not have avenged them herself? Did she not always remind the poet of Joan of Arc?

Another week passed; the shadow of the gallows crept over the days; on, on remorselessly drawing nearer, as the last ray of hope sank below the horizon. The Home Secretary remained inflexible; the great petitions discharged their signatures at him in vain. He was a Conservative, sternly conscientious; and the mere insinuation that his obstinacy was due to the politics of the condemned only hardened him against the temptation of a cheap reputation for magnanimity. He would not even grant a respite, to increase the chances of the discovery of Jessie Dymond. In the last of the three weeks there was a final monster meeting of protest. Grodman again took the chair, and several distinguished faddists were present, as well as numerous respectable members of society. The Home Secretary acknowledged the receipt of their resolutions. The Trade Unions were divided in their allegiance; some whispered of faith and hope, others of financial defalcations. The former essayed to organize a procession and an indignation meeting on the Sunday preceding the Tuesday fixed for the execution, but it fell through on a rumor of confession.

The Monday papers contained a last masterly letter from Grodman exposing the weakness of the evidence, but they knew nothing of a confession. The prisoner was mute and disdainful, professing little regard for a life empty of love and burdened with self-reproach. He refused to see clergymen. He was accorded an interview with Miss Brent in the presence of a gaoler, and solemnly asseverated his respect for her dead lover's memory. Monday buzzed with rumors; the evening papers chronicled them hour by hour. A poignant anxiety was abroad. The girl would be found. Some miracle would happen. A reprieve would arrive. The sentence would be commuted. But the short day darkened into night even as Mortlake's short day was darkening. And the shadow of the gallows crept on and on, and seemed to mingle with the twilight.

Crowl stood at the door of his shop, unable to work. His big grey eyes were heavy with unshed tears. The dingy wintry road seemed one vast cemetery; the street lamps twinkled like corpse-lights. The confused sounds of the street life reached his ear as from another world. He did not see the people who flitted to and fro amid the gathering shadows of the cold, dreary night. One ghastly vision flashed and faded and flashed upon the background of the duskiness.

Denzil stood beside him, smoking in silence. A cold fear was at his heart. That terrible Grodman! As the hangman's cord was tightening round Mortlake, he felt the convict's chains tightening round himself. And yet there was one gleam of hope, feeble as the yellow flicker of the gas lamp across the way. Grodman had obtained an interview with the condemned late that afternoon, and the parting had been painful, but the evening paper that in its turn had obtained an interview with the ex-detective, announced on its placard "GRODMAN STILL CONFIDENT" and the thousands who yet pinned their faith on this extraordinary man refused to extinguish the last sparks of hope. Denzil had bought the paper and scanned it eagerly, but there was nothing save the vague assurance that the indefatigable Grodman was still almost pathetically expectant of the miracle. Denzil did not share the expectation; he meditated flight.

"Peter," he said at last, "I'm afraid it's all over."

Crowl nodded, heart-broken. "All over!" he repeated, "and to think that he dies - and it is - all over!"

He looked despairingly at the blank winter sky, where leaden clouds shut out the stars. "Poor, poor young fellow! Tonight - alive and thinking. Tomorrow night - a clod, with no more sense or motion than a bit of leather! No compensation nowhere for being cut off innocent in the pride of youth and strength! A man who has always preached the Useful day and night, and toiled and suffered for his fellows. Where's the justice of it, where's the justice of it?" he demanded fiercely. Again his wet eyes wandered upwards towards heaven, that heaven away from which the soul of a dead saint at the Antipodes was speeding into infinite space.

"Well, where was the justice for Arthur Constant if he too was innocent?" said Denzil. "Really, Peter, I don't see why you should take it for granted that Tom is so dreadfully injured. Your horny handed labor leaders are, after all, men of no aesthetic refinement, with no sense of the Beautiful; you cannot expect them to be exempt from the coarser forms of crime. Humanity must look to far other leaders - to the seers and the poets!"

"Cantercot, if you say Tom's guilty I'll knock you down." The little cobbler turned upon his tall friend like a roused lion. Then he added, "I beg your pardon, Cantercot, I don't mean that. After all, I've no grounds. The judge is an honest man, and with gifts I can't lay claim to. But I believe in Tom with all my heart. And if Tom is guilty I believe in the Cause of the People with all my heart all the same. The Fads are doomed to death; they may be reprieved, but they must die at last."

He drew a deep sigh, and looked along the dreary Road. It was quite dark now, but by the light of the lamps and the gas in the shop windows the dull, monotonous Road lay revealed in all its sordid, familiar outlines; with its long stretches of chill pavement, its unlovely architecture, and its endless stream of prosaic pedestrians.

A sudden consciousness of the futility of his existence pierced the little cobbler like an icy wind. He saw his own life, and a hundred million lives like his, swelling and breaking like bubbles on a dark ocean, unheeded, uncared for.

A newsboy passed along, clamoring "The Bow murderer, preparaitions for the hexecution!"

A terrible shudder shook the cobbler's frame. His eyes ranged sightlessly after the boy; the merciful tears filled them at last.

"The Cause of the People," he murmured brokenly, "I believe in the Cause of the People. There is nothing else."

"Peter, come in to tea, you'll catch cold," said Mrs. Crowl.

Denzil went in to tea and Peter followed.

Meantime, round the house of the Home Secretary, who was in town, an ever-augmenting crowd was gathered, eager to catch the first whisper of a reprieve.

The house was guarded by a cordon of police, for there was no inconsiderable danger of a popular riot. At times a section of the crowd groaned and hooted. Once a volley of stones was discharged at the windows. The newsboys were busy vending their special editions, and the reporters struggled through the crowd, clutching descriptive pencils, and ready to rush off to telegraph offices should anything "extra special" occur. Telegraph boys were coming up every now and again with threats, messages, petitions and exhortations from all parts of the country to the unfortunate Home Secretary, who was striving to keep his aching head cool as he went through the voluminous evidence for the last time and pondered over the more important letters which "The Greater Jury" had contributed to the obscuration of the problem. Grodman's letter in that morning's paper shook him most; under his scientific analysis the circumstantial chain seemed forged of painted cardboard. Then the poor man read the judge's summing up, and the chain became tempered steel. The noise of the crowd outside broke upon his ear in his study like the roar of a distant ocean. The more the rabble hooted him, the more he essayed to hold scrupulously the scales of life and death. And the crowd grew and grew, as men came away from their work. There were many that loved the man who lay in the jaws of death, and a spirit of mad revolt surged in their breasts. And the sky was grey, and the bleak night deepened, and the shadow of the gallows crept on.

Suddenly a strange inarticulate murmur spread through the crowd, a vague whisper of no one knew what. Something had happened. Somebody was coming. A second later and one of the outskirts of the throng was agitated, and a convulsive cheer went up from it, and was taken up infectiously all along the street. The crowd parted; a hansom dashed through the center.

"Grodman! Grodman!" shouted those who recognized the occupant. "Grodman! Hurrah!" Grodman was outwardly calm and pale, but his eyes glittered; he waved his hand encouragingly as the hansom dashed up to the door, cleaving the turbulent crowd as a canoe cleaves the waters. Grodman sprang out, the constables at the portal made way for him respectfully. He knocked imperatively, the door was opened cautiously; a boy rushed up and delivered a telegram; Grodman forced his way in, gave his name, and insisted on seeing the Home Secretary on a matter of life and death. Those near the door heard his words and cheered, and the crowd divined the good omen, and the air throbbed with cannonades of joyous sound. The cheers rang in Grodman's ears as the door slammed behind him. The reporters struggled to the front. An excited knot of working men pressed round the arrested hansom; they took the horse out. A dozen enthusiasts struggled for the honor of placing themselves between the shafts. And the crowd awaited Grodman.

XII

Grodman was ushered into the conscientious Minister's study. The doughty chief of the agitation was perhaps the one man who could not be denied. As he entered, the Home Secretary's face seemed lit up with relief. At a sign from his master, the amanuensis who had brought in the last telegram took it back with him into the outer room where he worked. Needless to say not a tithe of the Minister's correspondence ever came under his own eyes.

"You have a valid reason for troubling me, I suppose, Mr. Grodman?" said the Home Secretary, almost cheerfully. "Of course it is about Mortlake?"

"It is; and I have the best of all reasons."

"Take a seat. Proceed."

"Pray do not consider me impertinent, but have you ever given any attention to the science of evidence?"

"How do you mean?" asked the Home Secretary, rather puzzled, adding, with a melancholy smile, "I have had to lately. Of course, I've never been a criminal lawyer, like some of my predecessors. But I should hardly speak of it as a science; I look upon it as a question of common sense."

"Pardon me, sir. It is the most subtle and difficult of all the sciences. It is, indeed, rather the science of the sciences. What is the whole of Inductive Logic, as laid down, say, by Bacon and Mill, but an attempt to appraise the value of evidence, the said evidence being the trails left by the Creator, so to speak? The Creator has - I say it in all reverence - drawn a myriad red herrings across the track but the true scientist refuses to be baffled by superficial appearances in detecting the secrets of Nature. The vulgar herd catches at the gross apparent fact, but the man of insight knows that what lies on the surface does lie."

"Very interesting, Mr. Grodman, but really..."

"Bear with me, sir. The science of evidence being thus so extremely subtle, and demanding the most acute and trained observation of facts, the most comprehensive understanding of human psychology, is naturally given over to professors who have not the remotest idea that 'things are not what they seem,' and that everything is other than it appears; to professors, most of whom by their year long devotion to the shop counter or the desk, have acquired an intimate acquaintance with all the infinite shades and complexities of things and human nature. When twelve of these professors are put in a box, it is called a jury. When one of these professors is put in a box by himself, he is called a witness. The retailing of evidence - the observation of the facts - is given over to people who go through their lives without eyes; the appreciation of evidence - the judging of these facts - is surrendered to people who may possibly be adepts in weighing out pounds of sugar. Apart from their sheer inability to fulfill either function - to observe, or to judge – their observation and their judgment alike are vitiated by all sorts of irrelevant prejudices."

"You are attacking trial by jury."

"Not necessarily. I am prepared to accept that scientifically, on the ground that, as there are, as a rule, only two alternatives, the balance of probability is slightly in favor of the true decision being come to. Then, in cases where experts like myself have got up the evidence, the jury can be made to see through trained eyes."

The Home Secretary tapped impatiently with his foot.

"I can't listen to abstract theorizing," he said. "Have you any fresh concrete evidence?"

"Sir, everything depends on our getting down to the root of the matter. What percentage of average evidence should you think is thorough, plain, simple, unvarnished fact, 'the truth, the whole truth, and nothing but the truth'?"

"Fifty?" said the Minister, humoring him a little.

"Not five. I say nothing of lapses of memory, of inborn defects of observational power; though the suspiciously precise recollection of dates and events possessed by ordinary witnesses in important trials taking place years after the occurrences involved is one of the most amazing things in the curiosities of modern jurisprudence. I defy you, sir, to tell me what you had for dinner last Monday, or what exactly you were saying and doing at five o'clock last Tuesday afternoon. Nobody whose life does not run in mechanical grooves can do anything of the sort; unless, of course, the facts have been very impressive. But this by the way. The great obstacle to veracious observation is the element of prepossession in all vision. Has it ever struck you sir, that we never *see* anyone more than once, if that? The first time we meet a man we may possibly see him as he is; the second time our vision is colored and modified by the memory of the first. Do our friends appear to us as they appear to strangers? Do our rooms, our furniture, our pipes strike our eye as they would strike the eye of an outsider, looking on them for the first time? Can a mother see her babe's ugliness, or a lover his mistress's shortcomings, though they stare everybody else in the face? Can we see ourselves as others see us? No; habit, prepossession changes all. The mind is a large factor of every so-called external fact. The eye sees, sometimes, what it wishes to see, more often what it expects to see. You follow me, sir?"

The Home Secretary nodded his head less impatiently. He was beginning to be interested. The hubbub from without broke faintly upon their ears.

"To give you a definite example. Mr. Wimp says that when I burst open the door of Mr. Constant's room on the morning of December 4th, and saw that the staple of the bolt had been wrested by the pin from the lintel, I jumped at once to the conclusion that I had broken the bolt. Now I admit that this was so, only in things like this you do not seem to *conclude*, you jump so fast that you *see*, or seem to. On the other hand, when you *see* a *standing* ring of fire produced by whirling a burning stick, you do *not* believe in its continuous existence. It is the same when witnessing a legerdemain performance. Seeing is not always believing, despite the proverb; but believing is often seeing. It is not to the point that in that little matter of the door Wimp was as hopelessly and incurably wrong as he has been in everything all along. The door *was* securely bolted. Still I confess that I should have seen that I had broken the bolt in forcing the door, even if it had been broken beforehand. Never once since December 4th did this possibility occur to me, till Wimp with perverted ingenuity suggested it. If this is the case with a trained observer, one moreover fully conscious of this ineradicable tendency of the human mind, how must it be with an untrained observer?"

"Come to the point. Come to the point," said the Home Secretary, putting out his hand as if it itched to touch the bell on the writing table.

"Such as," went on Grodman, imperturbably, "such as Mrs. Drabdump. That worthy person is unable, by repeated violent knocking, to arouse her lodger who yet desires to be aroused; she becomes alarmed, she rushes across to get my assistance; I burst open the door. What do you think the good lady expected to see?"

"Mr. Constant murdered, I suppose," murmured the Home Secretary, wonderingly.

"Exactly. And so she saw it. And what should you think was the condition of Arthur Constant when the door yielded to my violent exertions and flew open?"

"Why, was he not dead?" gasped the Home Secretary, his heart fluttering violently.

"Dead? A young, healthy fellow like that! When the door flew open, Arthur Constant was sleeping the sleep of the just. It was a deep, a very deep sleep, of course, else the blows at his door would long since have awakened him. But all the while Mrs. Drabdump's fancy was picturing her lodger cold and stark, the poor young fellow was lying in bed in a nice warm sleep."

"You mean to say you found Arthur Constant alive?"

"As you were last night."

The Minister was silent, striving confusedly to take in the situation. Outside the crowd was cheering again. It was probably to pass the time.

"Then, when was he murdered?"

"Immediately afterwards."

"By whom?"

"Well, that is, if you will pardon me, not a very intelligent question. Science and common sense are in accord for once. Try the method of exhaustion. It must have been either by Mrs. Drabdump or myself."

"You mean to say that Mrs. Drabdump...!"

"Poor dear Mrs. Drabdump, you don't deserve this of your Home Secretary! The idea of that good lady!"

"It was *you*!"

"Calm yourself, my dear Home Secretary. There is nothing to be alarmed at. It was a solitary experiment, and I intend it to remain so." The noise without grew louder. "Three cheers for Grodman! Hip, hip, hip, hooray," fell faintly on their ears.

But the Minister, pallid and deeply moved, touched the bell. The Home Secretary's home secretary appeared. He looked at the great man's agitated face with suppressed surprise.

"Thank you for calling in your amanuensis," said Grodman. "I intended to ask you to lend me his services. I suppose he can write shorthand."

The Minister nodded, speechless.

"That is well. I intend this statement to form the basis of an appendix to the twenty-fifth edition - sort of silver wedding - of my book, *Criminals I have Caught*. Mr. Denzil Cantercot, who, by the will I have made today, is appointed my literary executor, will have the task of working it up with literary and dramatic touches after the model of the other chapters of my book. I have every confidence he will be able to do me as much justice, from a literary point of view, as you sir, no doubt will from a legal. I feel certain he will succeed in catching the style of the other chapters to perfection."

"Templeton," whispered the Home Secretary, "this man may be a lunatic. The effort to solve the Big Bow Mystery may have addled his brain. Still," he added aloud, "it will be as well for you to take down his statement in shorthand."

"Thank you, sir," said Grodman heartily. "Ready, Mr. Templeton? Here goes. My career till I left the Scotland Yard Detective Department is known to all the world. Is that too fast for you, Mr. Templeton? A little? Well, I'll go slower; but pull me up if I forget to keep the brake on. When I retired, I discovered that I was a bachelor. But it was too late to marry. Time hung heavy on my hands. The preparation of my book, *Criminals I have Caught,* kept me occupied for some months. When it was published, I had nothing more to do but think. I had plenty of money, and it was safely invested; there was no call for speculation. The future was meaningless to me; I regretted I had not elected to die in harness. As idle old men must, I lived in the past. I went over and over again my ancient exploits; I re-read my book. And as I thought and thought, away from the excitement of the actual hunt, and seeing the facts in a truer perspective, so it grew daily clearer to me that criminals were more fools than rogues. Every crime I had traced, however cleverly perpetrated, was from the point of view of penetrability a weak failure. Traces and trails were left on all sides - ragged edges, rough-hewn corners; in short, the job was botched, artistic completeness unattained. To the vulgar, my feats might seem marvelous. The average man is mystified to grasp how you detect the letter 'e' in a simple cryptogram. To myself, they were as commonplace as the crimes they unveiled. To me now, with my lifelong study of the science of evidence, it seemed possible to commit not merely one but a thousand crimes that should be absolutely undiscoverable. And yet criminals would go on sinning, and giving themselves away, in the same old grooves - no originality, no dash, no individual insight, no fresh conception! One would imagine there were an Academy of crime with forty thousand armchairs.

And gradually, as I pondered and brooded over the thought, there came upon me the desire to commit a crime that should baffle detection. I could invent hundreds of such crimes, and please myself by imagining them done; but would they really work out in practice? Evidently the sole performer of my experiment must be myself; the subject - whom or what? Accident should determine. I itched to commence with murder - to tackle the stiffest problems first and I burned to startle and baffle the world - especially the world of which I had ceased to be. Outwardly I was calm, and spoke to the people about me as usual. Inwardly I was on fire with a consuming scientific passion. I sported with my pet theories and fitted them mentally on every one I met. Every friend or acquaintance I sat and gossiped with, I was plotting how to murder without leaving a clue. There is not one of my friends or acquaintances I have not done away with in thought. There is no public man - have no fear, my dear Home Secretary - I have not planned to assassinate secretly, mysteriously, unintelligibly, undiscoverably. Ah, how I could give the stock criminals points; with their secondhand motives, their conventional conceptions, their commonplace details, their lack of artistic feeling and restraint."

The crowd had again started cheering. Impatient as the watchers were, they felt that no news was good news. The longer the interview accorded by the Home Secretary to the chairman of the Defense Committee, the greater the hope his obduracy was melting. The idol of the people would be saved, and "Grodman" and "Tom Mortlake" were mingled in the exultant plaudits.

"The late Arthur Constant," continued the great criminologist, "came to live nearly opposite me. I cultivated his acquaintance; he was a lovable young fellow, an excellent subject for experiment. I do not know when I have ever taken to a man more. From the moment I first set eyes on him, there was a peculiar sympathy between us. We were drawn to each other. I felt instinctively he would be the man. I loved to hear him speak enthusiastically of the Brotherhood of Man - I, who knew the brotherhood of man was to the ape, the serpent, and the tiger - and he seemed to find a pleasure in stealing a moment's chat with me from his engrossing self-appointed duties. It is a pity humanity should have been robbed of so valuable a life. But it had to be. At a quarter to ten on the night of December 3rd he came to me. Naturally I said nothing about this visit at the inquest or the trial. His object was to consult me mysteriously about some girl. He said he had privately lent her money, which she was to repay at her convenience. What the money was for he did not know, except that it was somehow connected with an act of abnegation in which he had vaguely encouraged her. The girl had since disappeared, and he was in distress about her. He would not tell me who it was - of course now, sir, you know as well as I it was Jessie Dymond - but asked for advice as to how to set about finding her. He mentioned that Mortlake was leaving for Devonport by the first train on the next day. Of old I should have connected these two facts and sought the thread; now, as he spoke, all my thoughts were dyed red. He was suffering perceptibly from toothache, and in answer to my sympathetic inquiries told me it had been allowing him very little sleep. Everything combined to invite the trial of one of my favorite theories.

I spoke to him in a fatherly way, and when I had tendered some vague advice about the girl, I made him promise to secure a night's rest (before he faced the arduous tram-men's meeting in the morning) by taking a sleeping draught. I gave him a quantity of sulfonal in a phial. It is a new drug, which produces protracted sleep without disturbing digestion, and which I use myself. He promised faithfully to take the draught; and I also exhorted him earnestly to bolt and bar and lock himself in so as to stop up every chink or aperture by which the cold air of the winter's night might creep into the room. I remonstrated with him on the careless manner he treated his body, and he laughed in his good-humored, gentle way, and promised to obey me in all things. And he did. That Mrs. Drabdump, failing to rouse him, would cry 'Murder!' I took for certain. She is built that way. As even Sir Charles Brown-Harland remarked, she habitually takes her prepossessions for facts, her inferences for observations. She forecasts the future in grey. Most women of Mrs. Drabdump's class would have behaved as she did. She happened to be a peculiarly favorable specimen for working on by 'suggestion,' but I would have undertaken to produce the same effect on almost any woman. The key to the Big Bow Mystery is feminine psychology. The only uncertain link in the chain was, would Mrs. Drabdump rush across to get *me* to break open the door? Women always rush for a man. I was well nigh the nearest, and certainly the most authoritative man in the street, and I took it for granted she would."

"But suppose she hadn't?" the Home Secretary could not help asking.

"Then the murder wouldn't have happened, that's all. In due course Arthur Constant would have awoke, or somebody else breaking open the door would have found him sleeping; no harm done, nobody any the wiser. I could hardly sleep myself that night. The thought of the extraordinary crime I was about to commit - a burning curiosity to know whether Wimp would detect *the modus operandi* - the prospect of sharing the feelings of murderers with whom I had been in contact all my life without being in touch with the terrible joys of their inner life - the fear lest I should be too fast asleep to hear Mrs. Drabdump's knock - these things agitated me and disturbed my rest. I lay tossing on my bed, planning every detail of poor Constant's end. The hours dragged slowly and wretchedly on towards the misty dawn. I was racked with suspense. Was I to be disappointed after all? At last the welcome sound came - the rat-tat-tat of murder.

The echoes of that knock are yet in my ear. 'Come over and kill him!' I put my night-capped head out of the window and told her to wait for me. I dressed hurriedly, took my razor, and went across to 11 Glover Street. As I broke open the door of the bedroom in which Arthur Constant lay sleeping, his head resting on his hands, I cried, 'My God!' as if I saw some awful vision. A mist as of blood swam before Mrs. Drabdump's eyes. She cowered back, for an instant (I divined rather than saw the action) she shut off the dreaded sight with her hands. In that instant I had made my cut - precisely, scientifically - made so deep a cut and drawn out the weapon so sharply that there was scarce a drop of blood on it; then there came from the throat a jet of blood which Mrs. Drabdump, conscious only of the horrid gash, saw but vaguely. I covered up the face quickly with a handkerchief to hide any convulsive distortion. But as the medical evidence (in this detail accurate) testified, death was instantaneous. I pocketed the razor and the empty sulfonal phial. With a woman like Mrs. Drabdump to watch me, I could do anything I pleased. I got her to draw my attention to the fact that both the windows were fastened.

Some fool, by the by, thought there was a discrepancy in the evidence because the police found only one window fastened, forgetting that, in my innocence I took care not to refasten the window I had opened to call for aid. Naturally I did not call for aid before a considerable time had elapsed. There was Mrs. Drabdump to quiet, and the excuse of making notes as an old hand. My object was to gain time. I wanted the body to be fairly cold and stiff before being discovered, though there was not much danger here; for, as you saw by the medical evidence, there is no telling the time of death to an hour or two. The frank way in which I said the death was very recent disarmed all suspicion, and even Dr. Robinson was unconsciously worked upon, in adjudging the time of death, by the knowledge (query here, Mr. Templeton) that it had preceded my advent on the scene.

"Before leaving Mrs. Drabdump, there is just one point I should like to say a word about. You have listened so patiently, sir, to my lectures on the science of sciences that you will not refuse to hear the last. A good deal of importance has been attached to Mrs. Drabdump's oversleeping herself by half an hour. It happens that this (like the innocent fog which has also been made responsible for much) is a purely accidental and irrelevant circumstance. In all works on inductive logic it is thoroughly recognized that only some of the circumstances of a phenomenon are of its essence and casually interconnected; there is always a certain proportion of heterogeneous accompaniments which have no intimate relation whatever with the phenomenon. Yet, so crude is as yet the comprehension of the science of evidence, that *every* feature of the phenomenon under investigation is made equally important, and sought to be linked with the chain of evidence. To attempt to explain everything is always the mark of the tyro. The fog and Mrs. Drabdump's oversleeping herself were mere accidents. There are always these irrelevant accompaniments, and the true scientist allows for this element of (so to speak) chemically unrelated detail. Even I never counted on the unfortunate series of accidental phenomena which have led to Mortlake's implication in a network of suspicion. On the other hand, the fact that my servant, Jane, who usually goes about ten, left a few minutes earlier on the night of December 3rd, so that she didn't know of Constant's visit, was a relevant accident. In fact, just as the art of the artist or the editor consists largely in knowing what to leave out, so does the art of the scientific detector of crime consist in knowing what details to ignore. In short, to explain everything is to explain too much. And too much is worse than too little.

"To return to my experiment. My success exceeded my wildest dreams. None had an inkling of the truth. The insolubility of the Big Bow Mystery teased the acutest minds in Europe and the civilized world. That a man could have been murdered in a thoroughly inaccessible room savored of the ages of magic. The redoubtable Wimp, who had been blazoned as my successor, fell back on the theory of suicide. The mystery would have slept till my death, but - I fear - for my own ingenuity. I tried to stand outside myself, and to look at the crime with the eyes of another, or of my old self. I found the work of art so perfect as to leave only one sublimely simple solution. The very terms of the problem were so inconceivable that, had I not been the murderer, I should have suspected myself, in conjunction, of course, with Mrs. Drabdump. The first persons to enter the room would have seemed to me guilty. I wrote at once (in a disguised hand and over the signature of 'One who Looks Through his Own Spectacles') to the *Pell Mell Press* to suggest this. By associating myself thus with Mrs. Drabdump I made it difficult for people to dissociate the two who entered the room together. To dash a half truth in the world's eyes is the surest way of blinding it altogether. This pseudonymous letter of mine, I contradicted (in my own name) the next day, and in the course of the long letter which I was tempted to write, I adduced fresh evidence against the theory of suicide. I was disgusted with the open verdict and wanted men to be up and doing and trying to find me out. I enjoyed the hunt more.

"Unfortunately, Wimp, set on the chase again by my own letter, by dint of persistent blundering, blundered into a track which - by a devilish tissue of coincidences I had neither foreseen nor dreamt of - seemed to the world the true. Mortlake was arrested and condemned. Wimp had apparently crowned his reputation. This was too much. I had taken all this trouble merely to put a feather in Wimp's cap, whereas I had expected to shake his reputation by it. It was bad enough that an innocent man should suffer; but that Wimp should achieve a reputation he did not deserve and overshadow all his predecessors by dint of a colossal mistake, this seemed to me intolerable. I have moved heaven and earth to get the verdict set aside, and to save the prisoner; I have exposed the weakness of the evidence; I have had the world searched for the missing girl; I have petitioned and agitated. In vain. I have failed. Now I play my last card. As the overweening Wimp could not be allowed to go down to posterity as the solver of this terrible mystery, I decided that the condemned man might just as well profit by his exposure. That is the reason I make the exposure tonight, before it is too late to save Mortlake."

"So that is the reason?" said the Home Secretary, with a suspicion of mockery in his tones.

"The sole reason."

Even as he spoke, a deeper roar than ever penetrated the study.

"A Reprieve! Hooray! Hooray!" The whole street seemed to rock with earthquake and the names of Grodman and Mortlake to be thrown up in a fiery jet. "A Reprieve! A Reprieve!" And then the very windows rattled with cheers for the Minister. And even above that roar rose the shrill voices of the newsboys, "Reprieve of Mortlake! Mortlake Reprieved!" Grodman looked wonderingly towards the street. "How do they know?" he murmured.

"Those evening papers are amazing," said the Minister, drily. "But I suppose they had everything ready in type for the contingency." He turned to his secretary.

"Templeton, have you got down every word of Mr. Grodman's confession?"

"Every word, sir."

"Then bring in the cable you received just as Mr. Grodman entered the house."

Templeton went back into the outer room and brought back the cablegram that had been lying on the Minister's writing table when Grodman came in. The Home Secretary silently handed it to his visitor. It was from the Chief of Police of Melbourne, announcing that Jessie Dymond had just arrived in that city in a sailing vessel, ignorant of all that had occurred, and had been immediately dispatched back to England, having made a statement entirely corroborating the theory of the defense.

"Pending further inquiries into this," said the Home Secretary not without appreciation of the grim humor of the situation as he glanced at Grodman's ashen cheeks, "I have reprieved the prisoner. Mr. Templeton was about to dispatch the messenger to the governor of Newgate as you entered this room. Mr. Wimp's card castle would have tumbled to pieces without your assistance. Your still undiscoverable crime would have shaken his reputation as you intended."

A sudden explosion shook the room and blent with the cheers of the populace. Grodman had shot himself, very scientifically, in the heart. He fell at the Home Secretary's feet, stone dead.

Some of the working men who had been standing waiting by the shafts of the hansom helped to bear the stretcher.

Israel Zangwill

CHEATING THE GALLOWS

Chapter 1: Curious Couple

They say that a union of opposites makes the happiest marriage, and perhaps it is on the same principle that men who chum are always so oddly assorted. You shall find a man of letters sharing diggings with an auctioneer, and a medical student pigging with a stockbroker's clerk. Perhaps each thus escapes the temptation to talk "shop" in his hours of leisure, while he supplements his own experiences of life by his companion's.

There could not be an odder couple than Tom Peters and Everard G. Roxdal - the contrast began with their names and ran through the entire chapter. They had a bedroom and a sitting room in common, but it would not be easy to find what else. To his landlady, worthy Mrs. Seacon, Tom Peters's profession was a little vague, but everybody knew that Roxdal was the manager of the City and Suburban Bank, and it puzzled her to think why a bank manager should live with such a seedy-looking person, who smoked clay pipes and sipped whiskey and water all the evening when he was at home. For Roxdal was as spruce and erect as his fellow lodger was round shouldered and shabby; he never smoked, and he confined himself to a small glass of claret at dinner.

It is possible to live with a man and see very little of him. Where each of the partners lives his own life in his own way, with his own circle of friends and external amusements, days may go by without the men having five minutes together. Perhaps this explains why these partnerships jog along so much more peaceably than marriages, where the chain is drawn so much tighter, and galls the partners rather than links them. Diverse, however, as were the hours and habits of the chums, they often breakfasted together and they agreed in one thing - they never stayed out at night. For the rest Peters sought his diversions in the company of journalists, and frequented debating rooms, where he propounded the most iconoclastic views; while Roxdal had highly respectable houses open to him in the suburbs and was, in fact, engaged to be married to Clara Newell, the charming daughter of a retired corn merchant, a widower with no other child.

Clara naturally took up a good deal of Roxdal's time, and he often dressed to go to the play with her, while Peters stayed at home in a faded dressing gown and loose slippers. Mrs. Seacon liked to see gentlemen about the house in evening dress and made comparisons not favorable to Peters. And this in spite of the fact that he gave her infinitely less trouble than the younger man. It was Peters who first took the apartments, and it was characteristic of his easy-going temperament that he was so openly and naïvely delighted with the view of the Thames obtainable from the bedroom window, that Mrs. Seacon was emboldened to ask twenty-five percent more than she had intended. She soon returned to her normal terms, however, when his friend Roxdal called the next day to inspect the rooms, and overwhelmed her with a demonstration of their numerous shortcomings. He pointed out that their being on the ground floor was not an advantage, but a disadvantage, since they were nearer the noises of the street, in fact, the house being a corner one, the noises of two streets. Roxdal continued to exhibit the same finicking temperament in the petty details of the ménage. His shirt fronts were never sufficiently starched, nor his boots sufficiently polished.

Tom Peters, having no regard for rigid linen, was always good-tempered and satisfied, and never acquired the respect of his landlady. He wore blue check shirts and loose ties even on Sundays. It is true he did net go to church, but slept on till Roxdal returned from morning service, and even then it was difficult to get him out of bed, or to make him hurry up his toilette operations. Often the midday meal would be smoking on the table while Peters would smoke in the bed, and Roxdal, with his head thrust through the folding doors that separated the bedroom from the sitting room, would be adjuring the sluggard to arise and shake off his slumbers and threatening to sit down without him, lest the dinner be spoilt. In revenge, Tom was usually up first on weekdays, sometimes at such unearthly hours that Polly had not yet removed the boots from outside the bedroom door, and would bawl down to the kitchen for his shaving water. For Tom, lazy and indolent as he was, shaved with the unfailing regularity of a man to whom shaving has become an instinct. If he had not kept fairly regular hours, Mrs. Seacon would have set him down as an actor, so clean shaven was he. Roxdal did not shave. He wore a full beard, and, being a fine figure of a man to boot, no uneasy investor could look upon him without being reassured as to the stability of the bank he managed so successfully. And thus the two men lived in an economical comradeship, all the firmer, perhaps, for their mutual incongruities.

Chapter 2: A Woman's Instinct

It was on a Sunday afternoon in the middle of October, ten days after Roxdal had settled in his new rooms, that Clara Newell paid her first visit to him there. She enjoyed a good deal of liberty, and did not mind accepting his invitation to tea. The corn merchant, himself indifferently educated, had an exaggerated sense of the value of culture, and so

Clara, who had artistic tastes without much actual talent, had gone in for painting and might be seen, in pretty toilettes, copying pictures in the Museum. At one time it looked as if she might be reduced to working seriously at her art for Satan, who finds mischief still for idle hands to do, had persuaded her father to embark the fruits of years of toil in bubble companies. However, things turned out not so bad as they might have been, a little was saved from the wreck and the appearance of a suitor, in the person of Everard G. Roxdal, ensured her a future of competence, if not the luxury she had been entitled to expect. She had a good deal of affection for Everard, who was unmistakably a clever man, as well as a good-looking one. The prospect seemed fair and cloudless. Nothing presaged the terrible storm that was about to break over these two lives. Nothing had ever for a moment come to vex their mutual contentment, till this Sunday afternoon. The October sky, blue and sunny, with an Indian summer sultriness, seemed an exact image of her life, with its aftermath of a happiness that had once seemed blighted.

Everard had always been so attentive, so solicitous, that she was as much surprised as chagrined to find that he had apparently forgotten the appointment. Hearing her astonished interrogation of Polly in the passage, Tom shambled from the sitting room in his loose slippers and his blue check shirt, with his eternal clay pipe in his mouth, and informed her that Roxdal had gone out suddenly earlier in the afternoon.

"G-g-one out," stammered poor Clara; all confused. "But he asked me to come to tea."

"Oh, you're Miss Newell, I suppose," said Tom.

"Yes, I am Miss Newell."

"He has told me a great deal about you, but I wasn't able honestly to congratulate him on his choice till now."

Clara blushed uneasily under the compliment, and under the ardor of his admiring gaze. Instinctively she distrusted the man. The very first tones of his deep bass voice gave her a peculiar shudder. And then his impoliteness in smoking that vile clay was so gratuitous.

"Oh, then you must be Mr. Peters," she said in return. "He has often spoken to me of you."

"Ah!" said Tom, laughingly, "I suppose he's told you all my vices. That accounts for your not being surprised at my Sunday attire."

She smiled a little, showing a row of pearly teeth. "Everard ascribes to you all the virtues," she said.

"Now that's what I call a friend!" he cried, ecstatically. "But won't you come in? He must be back in a moment. He surely would not break an appointment with you." The admiration latent in the accentuation of the last pronoun was almost offensive.

She shook her head. She had a just grievance against Everard, and would punish him by going away indignantly.

"Do let me give you a cup of tea," Tom pleaded. "You must be awfully thirsty this sultry weather. There! I will make a bargain with you! If you will come in now, I promise to clear out the moment Everard returns, and not spoil your tête-à-tête." But Clara was obstinate; she did not at all relish this man's society, and besides, she was not going to throw away her grievance against Everard. "I know Everard will slang me dreadfully when he comes in if I let you go," Tom urged. "Tell me at least where he can find you."

"I am going to take the 'bus at Charing Cross, and I'm going straight home," Clara announced determinedly. She put up her parasol in a pet, and went up the street into the Strand. A cold shadow seemed to have fallen over all things. But just as she was getting into the 'bus, a hansom dashed down Trafalgar Square, and a well-known voice hailed her. The hansom stopped, and Everard got out and held out his hand.

"I'm so glad you're a bit late," he said. "I was called out unexpectedly and have been trying to rush back in time. You wouldn't have found me if you had been punctual. But I thought," he added, laughing, "I could rely on you as a woman."

"I was punctual," Clara said angrily. "I was not getting out of this 'bus, as you seem to imagine, but into it, and was going home."

"My darling!" he cried remorsefully. "A thousand apologies." The regret on his handsome face soothed her. He took the rose he was wearing in the button-hole of his fashionably-cut coat and gave it to her.

"Why were you so cruel?" he murmured, as she nestled against him in the hansom. "Think of my despair if I had come home to hear you had come and gone. Why didn't you wait a moment?"

A shudder traversed her frame. "Not with that man, Peters!" she murmured.

"Not with that man, Peters!" he echoed sharply. "What is the matter with Peters?"

"I don't know," she said. "I don't like him."

"Clara," he said, half sternly, half cajolingly, "I thought you were above these feminine weaknesses; you are punctual, strive also to be reasonable. Tom is my best friend. From boyhood we have been always together. There is nothing Tom would not do for me, or I for Tom. You must like him, Clara; you must, if only for my sake."

"I'll try," Clara promised, and then he kissed her in gratitude and broad daylight.

"You'll be very nice to him at tea, won't you?" he said anxiously. "I shouldn't like you two to be bad friends."

"I don't want to be bad friends," Clara protested; "only the moment I saw him a strange repulsion and mistrust came over me."

"You are quite wrong about him - quite wrong," he assured her earnestly. "When you know him better, you'll find him the best of fellows. Oh, I know," he said suddenly, "I suppose he was very untidy, and you women go so much by appearances!"

"Not at all," Clara retorted. "'Tis you men who go by appearances."

"Yes, you do. That's why you care for me," he said, smiling.

She assured him it wasn't, and she didn't care for him so much as he plumed himself, but he smiled on. His smile died away, however, when he entered his rooms and found Tom nowhere.

"I daresay you've made him run about hunting for me," he grumbled.

"Perhaps he knew I'd come back, and went away to leave us together," she answered. "He said he would when you came."

"And yet you say you don't like him!"

She smiled reassuringly. Inwardly, however, she felt pleased at the man's absence.

Chapter 3: Polly Receives a Proposal

If Clara Newell could have seen Tom Peters carrying on with Polly in the passage, she might have felt justified in her prejudice against him. It must be confessed, though, that Everard also carried on with Polly. Alas! It is to be feared that men are much of a muchness where women are concerned; shabby men and smart men, bank managers and journalists, bachelors and semi-detached bachelors. Perhaps it was a mistake after all to say the chums had nothing patently in common. Everard, I am afraid, kissed Polly rather more often than Clara, and although it was because he respected her less, the reason would perhaps not have been sufficiently consoling to his affianced wife. For Polly was pretty, especially on alternate Sunday afternoons, and when at ten p.m. she returned from her outings, she was generally met in the passage by one or other of the men. Polly liked to receive the homage of real gentlemen, and set her white cap at all indifferently. Thus, just before Clara knocked on that memorable Sunday afternoon, Polly, being confined to the house by the unwritten code regulating the lives of servants, was amusing herself by flirting with Peters.

"You are fond of me a little bit," the graceless Tom whispered, "aren't you?"

"You know I am, sir," Polly replied.

"You don't care for anyone else in the house?"

"Oh no, sir, and never let anyone kiss me but you. I wonder how it is, sir?" Polly replied ingenuously.

"Give me another," Tom answered.

She gave him another, and tripped to the door to answer Clara's knock.

And that very evening, when Clara was gone and Tom still out, Polly turned without the faintest atom of scrupulosity, or even jealousy, to the more fascinating Roxdal, and accepted his amorous advances. If it would seem at first sight that Everard had less excuse for such frivolity than his friend, perhaps the seriousness he showed in this interview may throw a different light upon the complex character of the man.

"You're quite sure you don't care for anyone but me?" he asked earnestly.

"Of course not, sir!" Polly replied indignantly. "How could I?"

"But you care for that soldier I saw you out with last Sunday?"

"Oh no, sir, he's only my young man," she said apologetically.

"Would you give him up?" he hissed suddenly.

Polly's pretty face took a look of terror. "I couldn't, sir! He'd kill me. He's such a jealous brute, you've no idea."

"Yes, but suppose I took you away from here?" he whispered eagerly. "Somewhere where he couldn't find you; South America, Africa, somewhere thousands of miles across the seas."

"Oh sir, you frighten me!" whispered Polly, cowering before his ardent eyes, which shone in the dimly-lit passage.

"Would you come with me?" he hissed. She did not answer; she shook herself free and ran into the kitchen, trembling with a vague fear.

Chapter 4: The Crash

One morning, earlier than his earliest hour of demanding his shaving water, Tom rang the bell violently and asked the alarmed Polly what had become of Mr. Roxdal.

"How should I know, sir?" she gasped. "Ain't he been in, sir?"

"Apparently not," Tom answered anxiously. "He never remains out. We have been here three weeks now and I can't recall a single night he hasn't been home before twelve. I can't make it out." All enquiries proved futile. Mrs. Seacon reminded him of the thick fog that had come on suddenly the night before.

"What fog?" asked Tom.

"Lord! Didn't you notice it, sir?"

"No, I came in early, smoked, read and went to bed about eleven. I never thought of looking out of the window."

"It began about ten," said Mrs. Seacon, "and got thicker and thicker. I couldn't see the lights of the river from my bedroom. The poor gentleman has been and gone and walked into the water." She began to whimper.

"Nonsense, nonsense," said Tom, though his expression belied his words. "At the worst I should think he couldn't find his way home, and couldn't get a cab, so put up for the night at some hotel. I daresay it will be all right." He began to whistle as if in restored cheerfulness. At eight o'clock there came a letter for Roxdal, marked "immediate," but as he did not turn up for breakfast, Tom went round personally to the City and Suburban Bank. He waited half-an-hour there, but the manager did not make his appearance. Then he left the letter with the cashier and went away with anxious countenance.

That afternoon it was all over London that the manager of the City and Suburban had disappeared, and that many thousand pounds of gold and notes had disappeared with him.

Scotland Yard opened the letter marked "immediate," and noted that there had been a delay in its delivery, for the address had been obscure and an official alteration had been made. It was written in a feminine hand and said: "On second thoughts I cannot accompany you. Do not try to see me again. Forget me. I shall never forget you."

There was no signature.

Clara Newell, distracted, disclaimed all knowledge of this letter. Polly deposed that the fugitive had proposed flight to her and the routes to Africa and South America were especially watched. Some months passed without result. Tom Peters went about overwhelmed with grief and astonishment. The police took possession of all the missing man's effects. Gradually the hue and cry dwindled, died.

Chapter 5: Faith and Unfaith

"At last we meet!" cried Tom Peters, while his face lit up in joy. "How are you, dear Miss Newell?" Clara greeted him coldly. Her face had an abiding pallor now. Her lover's flight and shame had prostrated her for weeks. Her soul was the arena of contending instincts. Alone of all the world she still believed in Everard's innocence, felt that there was something more than met the eye, divined some devilish mystery behind it all. And yet that damning letter from the anonymous lady shook her sadly. Then, too, there was the deposition of Polly. When she heard Peters's voice accosting her all her old repugnance resurged. It flashed upon her that this man - Roxdal's boon companion - must know far more than he had told to the police. She remembered how Everard had spoken of him, with what affection and confidence! Was it likely he was utterly ignorant of Everard's movements? Mastering her repugnance, she held out her hand. It might be well to keep in touch with him; he was possibly the clue to the mystery. She noticed he was dressed a shade more trimly, and was smoking a meerschaum. He walked along at her side, making no offer to put his pipe out.

"You have not heard from Everard?" he asked. She flushed. "Do you think I'm an accessory after the fact?" she cried.

"No, no," he said soothingly. "Pardon me, I was thinking he might have written; giving no exact address, of course. Men do sometimes dare to write thus to women. But, of course, he knows you too well. You would have put the police on his track."

"Certainly," she exclaimed, indignantly. "Even if he is innocent he must face the charge."

"Do you still entertain the possibility of his innocence?"

"I do," she said boldly, and looked him full in the face. His eyelids drooped with a quiver. "Don't you?"

"I have hoped against hope," he replied in a voice faltering with emotion. "Poor old Everard! But I am afraid there is no room for doubt. Oh, this wicked curse of money tempting the noblest and the best of us."

The weeks rolled on. Gradually she found herself seeing more and more of Tom Peters, and gradually, strange to say, he grew less repulsive. From the talks they had together, she began to see that there was really no reason to put faith in Everard; his criminality, his faithlessness, were too flagrant. Gradually she grew ashamed of her early mistrust of Peters; remorse bred esteem, and esteem ultimately ripened into feelings so warm, that when Tom gave freer vent to the love that had been visible to Clara from the first, she did not repulse him.

It is only in books that love lives forever. Clara, so her father thought, showed herself a sensible girl in plucking out an unworthy affection and casting it from her heart. He invited the new lover to his house, and took to him at once. Roxdal's somewhat supercilious manner had always jarred upon the unsophisticated corn merchant. With Tom the old man got on much better. While evidently quite as well informed and cultured as his whilom friend, Tom knew how to impart his superior knowledge with the accent on the knowledge rather than on the superiority, while he had the air of gaining much information in return. Those who are most conscious of defects of early education are most resentful of other people sharing their consciousness. Moreover, Tom's bonhomie was far more to the old fellow's liking than the studied politeness of his predecessor, so that on the whole Tom made more of a conquest of the father than of the daughter. Nevertheless, Clara was by no means unresponsive to Tom's affection, and when, after one of his visits to the house, the old man kissed her fondly and spoke of the happy turn things had taken and how, for the second time in their lives, things had mended when they seemed at their blackest, her heart swelled with a gush of gratitude and joy and tenderness; and she fell sobbing into her father's arms.

Tom calculated that he made a clear five hundred a year by occasional journalism, besides possessing some profitable investments which he had inherited from his mother, so that there was no reason for delaying the marriage. It was fixed for May Day, and the honeymoon was to be spent in Italy.

Chapter 6: The Dream and the Awakening

But Clara was not destined to happiness. From the moment she had promised herself to her first love's friend old memories began to rise up and reproach her. Strange thoughts stirred in the depths of her soul, and in the silent watches of the night she seemed to hear Everard's accents, charged with grief and upbraiding. Her uneasiness increased as her wedding day drew near. One night, after a pleasant afternoon spent in being rowed by Tom among the upper reaches of the Thames, she retired to rest full of vague forebodings. And she dreamt a terrible dream. The dripping form of Everard stood by her bedside, staring at her with ghastly eyes. Had he been drowned on the passage to his land of exile? Frozen with horror, she put the question.

"I have never left England!" the vision answered.

Her tongue clove to the roof of her mouth.

"Never left England?" she repeated, in tones which did not seem to be hers.

The wraith's stony eyes stared on, but there was silence.

"Where have you been then?" she asked in her dream.

"Very near you," came the answer.

"There has been foul play then!" she shrieked.

The phantom shook its head in doleful assent.

"I knew it!" she shrieked. "Tom Peters! Tom Peters has done away with you. Is it not he? Speak!"

"Yes, it is he, Tom Peters, whom I loved more than all the world."

Even in the terrible oppression of the dream she could not resist saying, woman-like:

"Did I not warn you against him?"

The phantom stared on silently and made no reply.

"But what was his motive?" she asked at length.

"Love of gold, and you. And you are giving yourself to him," it said sternly.

"No, no, Everard! I will not! I will not! I swear it! Forgive me!"

The spirit shook its head skeptically.

"You love him. Women are false; as false as men."

She strove to protest again, but her tongue refused its office.

"If you marry him, I shall always be with you! Beware!"

The dripping figure vanished as suddenly as it came, and Clara awoke in a cold perspiration. Oh, it was horrible! The man she had learnt to love, the murderer of the man she had learnt to forget! How her original prejudice had been justified! Distracted, shaken to her depths, she would not take counsel even of her father, but informed the police of her suspicions. A raid was made on Tom's rooms, and lo! The stolen notes were discovered in a huge bundle. It was found that he had several banking accounts, with a large, recently-paid amount in each bank. Tom was arrested.

Attention was now concentrated on the corpses washed up by the river. It was not long before the body of Roxdal came to shore, the face distorted almost beyond recognition by long immersion, but the clothes patently his, and a pocketbook in the breast-pocket removing the last doubt. Mrs. Seacon and Polly and Clara Newell all identified the body. Both juries returned a verdict of murder against Tom Peters, the recital of Clara's dream producing a unique impression in the court and throughout the country.

The theory of the prosecution was that Roxdal had brought home the money, whether to fly alone or to divide it, or whether even for some innocent purpose, as Clara believed, was immaterial. That Peters determined to have it all, that he had gone out for a walk with the deceased, and, taking advantage of the fog, had pushed him into the river, and that he was further impelled to the crime by love for Clara Newell, as was evident from his subsequent relations with her. The judge put on the black cap. Tom Peters was duly hung by the neck till he was dead.

Chapter 7: Brief Resume of the Culprit's Confession

When you all read this I shall be dead and laughing at you. I have been hung for my own murder. I am Everard G. Roxdal. I am also Tom Peters. We two were one. When I was a young man my moustache and beard wouldn't come. I bought false ones to improve my appearance. One day, after I had become manager of the City and Suburban Bank, I took off my beard and moustache at home, and then the thought crossed my mind that nobody would know me without them. I was another man. Instantly it flashed upon me that if I ran away from the Bank, that other man could be left in London, while the police were scouring the world for a non-existent fugitive. But this was only the crude germ of the idea. Slowly I matured my plan. The man who was going to be left in London must be known to a circle of acquaintance beforehand. It would be easy enough to masquerade in the evenings in my beardless condition, with other disguises of dress and voice. But this was not brilliant enough. I conceived the idea of living with him. It was Box and Cox reversed. We shared rooms at Mrs. Seacon's. It was a great strain, but it was only for a few weeks. I had trick clothes in my bedroom like those of quick-change artistes; in a moment I could pass from Roxdal to Peters and from Peters to Roxdal. Polly had to clean two pairs of boots a morning, cook two dinners, etc., etc. She and Mrs. Seacon saw one or the other of us every moment; it never dawned upon them they never saw us both together. At meals I would not be interrupted, ate off two plates, and conversed with my friend in loud tones. At other times we dined at different hours. On Sundays he was supposed to be asleep when I was in church. There is no landlady in the world to whom the idea would have occurred that one man was troubling himself to be two (and to pay for two, including washing). I worked up the idea of Roxdal's flight, asked Polly to go with me, manufactured that feminine letter that arrived on the morning of my disappearance. As Tom Peters I mixed with a journalistic set. I had another room where I kept the gold and notes till I mistakenly thought the thing had blown over. Unfortunately, returning from here on the night of my disappearance, with Roxdal's clothes in a bundle I intended to drop into the river, it was stolen from me in the fog, and the man into whose possession it ultimately came appears to have committed suicide. What, perhaps, ruined me was my desire to keep Clara's love, and to transfer it to the survivor. Everard told her I was the best of fellows. Once married to her, I would not have had much fear. Even if she had discovered the trick, a wife cannot give evidence against her husband, and often does not want to. I made none of the usual slips, but no man can guard against a girl's nightmare after a day up the river and a supper at the Star and Garter. I might have told the judge he was an ass, but then I should have had penal servitude for bank robbery, and that is worse than death. The only thing that puzzles me, though, is whether the law has committed murder or I suicide.